Allan McFadden trained as a secondary school music teacher and has worked as an actor, a theatre composer, director, pianist and teacher. With fellow Australian Peter Fleming, he has composed many musicals, among them *Air Heart; Madame De, Frank Christie Frank Clarke! and Noli Me Tangere.* A lover of fiction writing and fiction film/television, as he approached his sixty-ninth birthday he had a desire to write the stuff.

Chris Blackam and Ian Cook
—Blackie and Cookie—
great mates, who like to read.

Allan McFadden

AU REVOIR, MATE!

AUSTIN MACAULEY PUBLISHERS™
LONDON • CAMBRIDGE • NEW YORK • SHARJAH

Copyright © Allan McFadden 2022

The right of Allan McFadden to be identified as author of this work has been asserted by the author in accordance with sections 77 and 78 of the Copyright, Designs and Patents Act 1988.

All rights reserved. No part of this publication may be reproduced, stored in a retrieval system, or transmitted in any form or by any means, electronic, mechanical, photocopying, recording, or otherwise, without the prior permission of the publishers.

Any person who commits any unauthorised act in relation to this publication may be liable to criminal prosecution and civil claims for damages.

This is a work of fiction. Names, characters, businesses, places, events, locales, and incidents are either the products of the author's imagination or used in a fictitious manner. Any resemblance to actual persons, living or dead, or actual events is purely coincidental.

A CIP catalogue record for this title is available from the British Library.

ISBN 9781398441965 (Paperback)
ISBN 9781398441972 (ePub e-book)

www.austinmacauley.com

First Published 2022
Austin Macauley Publishers Ltd®
1 Canada Square
Canary Wharf
London
E14 5AA

My thanks go to: Chris Blackam, Ian Cook, Rowena Dawson, John Ellis, and Lori Jeffrey, for their positive comments, constructive ideas and encouragement. And to Bill Conn whose lessons in editing always ring in my ears.

Notes

All characters and situations in *"Au Revoir, Mate!"* are fictional. They bear no resemblance to anyone alive or dead. The areas and streets of Nice and Cannes exist, though the buildings occupied by the characters do not.

Au revoir (French) means 'farewell' or 'goodbye'.
Bon nuit (French) means 'goodnight'.
Dva (Czech) means 'two'.
Maman (French) means 'mother'.
Mate (Australian) is a term for a friend, though it can be used ironically.

Chapter 1

My name is Dougay Roberre. The name on my passport is Douglas Roberts. Neither name is really mine. I don't know what my real name is.

I was born here in France, I believe, about forty years ago. My passport says I'm forty-one, my birthday is listed as March 16.

At the age of three, I was taken, without warning, by my parents to Australia. There, they were placed into a witness protection program. It was soon after locating to Sydney, they destroyed all evidence of their French existence. I have no photographs of being held in the arms of loving grandparents or doting aunts.

I grew up in the land of drought, flood, fire and surf. It was a wonderful upbringing. Then again when you've never experienced anything else, what do you have to compare it to? No, it truly was wonderful. I do have photographs of *that* as evidence. There's a photograph of me sitting on the bonnet of my first car, proudly smiling; me trying to stuff a sausage on a slice of bread into my acne riddled face; and me standing next to my first surfboard with a beautiful teenage girl, whose name went the way of the surfboard.

As I approached my fortieth birthday, I became uneasy. It wasn't an overnight thing, and I don't believe it was the impending doom of suddenly finding myself on the wrong side of desirability, rather it was something internal, something from the gut. I'd always found it difficult to settle, after both my parents had passed on. Their deaths were natural, not associated with their sudden departure from Paris, or Lyon, or Marseilles. I also do not know where I was born or from where they fled.

This disconcerting feeling grew so much so, that four months ago—in February—I uprooted myself and returned here. There were no broken-hearted lovers left behind. A few drinking mates teased that I'd be back in the New Year. I celebrated my birthday—alone—in an unknown bar I stumbled across near to the hostel I was staying in.

I had owned a small apartment overlooking Bondi Beach, in Sydney's east, which I'd bought cheaply as a young man. The only sensible thing I'd ever done. Over time, the Sydney property market increased in value and with the money I made from its sale, I bought myself a similar place here in Nice—though this apartment doesn't overlook the sea. I couldn't afford that! Being mentally an Australian, who'd lived by the sea, the Riviera was the perfect fit for me—and Nice was the only place I could afford to live in, along the Cote d'Azur.

I bought the apartment ten weeks ago. I'd seen it online, along with two others in my price range, back in Sydney before I left. Once here, I inspected the three, though I knew the one I wanted. Yesterday, I took possession of it.

Somewhere in the middle of next month, my budgeted transitional money will run out. I'd opened a bank account when I arrived, depositing the balance, however, I now needed to find something to do and something that would pay. I was planning on keeping that deposit as a nest egg—even gradually building on it. I know the merits of saving, as opposed to living on credit. My parents taught me well about a great many things, though not my family history.

Because of my parents, I can speak excellent French, though I cannot read nor write it. Oh, the basic phrases I recognise, however I'll never have a job translating Moliere into English. I have no qualifications which are recognisable here in France. No qualifications which are recognisable in Australia for that matter. There, I'd always been a man-for-hire.

That is me—Dougay Roberre: *L'Homme Engager*.

When one relocates to a new country, it's hard to find a job at the top end of town. I was prepared to start at the bottom. I'm a realist—never thinking I'd stay down there forever. Whoever does?

My apartment is on the top floor of a Belle Epoque building on Avenue Auber, near Place Mozart, very near the T-junction with Rue Beethoven. Parallel to Avenue Auber runs Rue Gounod and across it runs Rue Rossini. Nearer the beach is Rue Saint-Saens. I'm not making up these street names. According to the agent, there are no buskers in the vicinity, as they are psychologically restrained from performing by the standard of musicianship inherent in the street names around them.

Place Mozart sounds as if it's a highly regarded, must-see oasis in the middle of the tourist bustle, a tribute to the boy-genius. It isn't. It is simply a square piece of grass over and around a car park. At the time, I didn't know that I would come to frequent it as often as I would and like anything through constant use, I'd come to regard it as a natural extension of my home.

My apartment was once two small attic studios. Someone had knocked out the wall and converted it into a reasonably sized two-bedroom loft. I'd carried in my two suitcases of clothing, unfurled my Australian sleeping bag and tossed it onto the floor of the bedroom on the right.

The whole place needed work—though the plumbing and electricity were operable; the roof didn't leak; and the floor didn't sag. Being a handyman—a jack-of-all-trades—I was looking forward to renovating it, bit by bit. First, I needed to buy a bed, a sofa, a table and chairs—second-hand, of course.

For the past ten weeks, waiting for the sale to be completed, I had walked these streets, getting a feel for the area I'd one day be living in. I bought a coffee each morning at a different café, hoping eventually to find the one I preferred. I didn't—I equally enjoyed them all. Until one morning, that is, when the simplest of gestures ended up cementing a relationship for the future.

At the pretentiously named *L'Opera Mozart*, the owner struggled clearing several tables.

"I'll take those for you." I held out my hand and after hesitating and giving me a curiously suspicious eye, he stacked five cups and saucers onto it. He gathered the remainder and I followed him inside. I placed them on the counter and turned to leave.

"Wait! You're not working this morning?" the owner asked.

"Oh—I'm looking for a job."

"My partner is ill." The proprietor went on to explain. "I need someone to do the washing up. Three days from nine until two; then seven until whenever. Cash in hand—no questions asked."

I thought about it, though not for long. "That's the best offer I've had in a long time," I said. "Lead me to the kitchen sink."

The café owner was Claude Tanguay—a pleasantly spoken and honest-faced man of fifty, with an overall cheery disposition. He was bald, with a wide row of hair above the ears and around the scalp. He had a natural air of 'mine host' about him and for the three days I worked there, he wore a black waistcoat over a white shirt—though every day the shirt was a fresh and neatly ironed one.

He paid me as promised on the evening of the third day. I was pleasantly surprised. I cannot tell you the number of times I've had to hassle for what is rightfully due me.

"Don't gamble it away." He smiled at his warning.

"No. Tomorrow I'm off to buy a bed," I explained. "I'll need every euro cent."

"What?" he questioned, curious that I'd lash out on something so mundane, though to me so necessary. I explained my newly arrived situation. He clicked his fingers. "My sister wants to get rid of a bed."

He made a phone call and I waited until he locked up the café and we walked off into the dark together. I had no idea where he led me—down streets and an alley way as a short cut—until we reached his sister's place.

We walked back carrying a wire bed frame to the foyer of my apartment block.

"You can't dump that in here!" the startled caretaker exclaimed. He was a small, nimble man in his sixties. His close-cropped hair was growing silver amongst the grey. Clean shaven, he obviously looked after himself, or a wife did, for his clothes, though casual, were ironed.

"Not dumping!" I reassured him. "I'll be sleeping on it tonight."

"Looks like you'll only get the one sleep out of that old thing." The caretaker had a sense of humour, as well as an astute eye.

"We'll just leave it here against the wall," I said. "We've got to go get the mattress."

Claude turned and I followed him to the front door.

"Non! Non!" shouted the caretaker after us.

We were out the door and, inside the hour, returned with the mattress. We ignored the old man sitting at his desk observing every move we made and headed to the old metal elevator. I slid the cage-like door, and we jammed the mattress in. I pushed the button for the top floor, and while the elevator rose, Claude and I climbed the stairs. Up there, we dragged out the mattress into my apartment.

Claude looked around at the barren rooms. "I know a man, who knows a man…" He told me of a friend who had a warehouse which contained lots of stuff—stuff that people no longer wanted; stuff that people couldn't sell; and stuff which had probably fallen off the backs of trucks. I said that tomorrow I'd pay him a visit.

Downstairs, I loaded the elevator with the bed frame and thanked Claude for all his help; told him to thank his sister for cancelling her twenty-euro asking price; and promised to become a regular customer at *L'Opera Mozart*.

Claude left waving, "*Adieu, mon ami!*"

"*Merci*, Claude!" I called after him, "Anytime you need help in your café, I'm your man!"

"Why don't you knock on the doors and wake *all* the tenants?" asked the caretaker, unimpressed with the noise I'd managed to create. He watched Claude disappear into the night. He turned to me. "A word of warning," he said.

I stopped by the elevator, waiting to be told how many rules and regulations I'd broken. The old man pointed after Claude, "The warning is—his coffee is watered down!" Then he laughed out loud.

I smiled appreciatively. "*Monsieur*, what's your name?

"Everyone calls me, M'sieur Pom!"

"Pleased to meet you, I am—"

"Dougay Roberre—from Australia."

*

Claude's friend was Remy Didion, who owned a warehouse, over the railway line in an area known as *Le Piol*. With my phone map as guide, I walked there and found it near the Cathedral Saint-Nicholas. It was a characterless building—a roller door for truck access; a cardboard covered large window; a heavy steel door for us pedestrians; and a lone CCTV camera fixed to the corner, covering both entrances. It was exactly what you'd want if there was anything dodgy attached to your business dealings.

Claude had told me Remy had been a boxer in his prime and his hands looked as if they still held a mean fist. That was what I saw first of him, as his handful of fingers gripped the steel door and opened it halfway. He peered around it and into the street behind me. He was suspicious. I'd found the right place.

"I'm Dougay Roberre. Claude told me to come."

"Claude? Which one? I know many Claudes."

"He's got the café over near Place Mozart."

The stockily framed man eyed me suspiciously. "Are you alone?"

I said I was. He slowly moved the door to let me in. "There are thieves about and these days, thieves can't be trusted." He locked it behind us. He turned on a switch and several overhead fluorescent strips spluttered into life, revealing a large warehouse.

Over to my left was a mezzanine level. I assumed that's where he slept. Perhaps there was a bathroom up there as well, down the back. Beneath it, on ground level in the corner, stood a large sink which seemed to be the collection point for all things liquid. Above the warehouse's low-slung lighting, it was hard to make out much of the detail up there on the mezzanine, as it all seemed to be embraced by collective gloom.

"Claude said you need some furniture," he said.

"I thought you didn't know *which* Claude?"

"It pays at first, not to know too much—about anything and anyone."

I told him what I was looking for. He walked by the various bits and pieces, and I pointed to what took my eye. As we passed, a large punching bag suspended from a hook, begged to be hit. I hit it.

"A straight left?" he said, and admiringly added, "And you know how to place your feet and turn your body sideways for protection."

I smiled and nodded. "Hope I didn't hurt your bag."

He laughed. "Where'd you learn that?"

"A friend of my father."

"The old skills—lost now. Idiots these days want to charge in, stand square and try to knock your head off. Or kick you in the guts. Kicking! When did that become an acceptable form of pugilism? Half the skill was dodging and weaving. The best fighters were the best dancers." He moved his head from side to side and threw a few air fists in my direction. He hadn't lost any of that skill.

"Maybe we could spar sometime," he suggested. "I need some exercise and you look like you could be worthwhile hitting." He laughed at his own joke. "Put out your left arm." I did. "You've a good reach. How's Saturday afternoons for you?"

"I have no gear. I'm as bereft of clothing as I am of furniture."

"What's this?" he asked. "Are you spinning me a tale of heartache?"

"No. I'm just being truthful."

He closed one eye, thinking. "Where's that slight accent from?"

"Is it noticeable? Australia."

"Ah well," he conceded. "If you can't hit, I suppose you can skip." He made out like a boxing kangaroo and laughed. "Don't worry, I've got all the gear you'll need, including smelling salts and a stretcher." He laughed again.

"I'll think about it." I could possibly tolerate his punches, however his wit, I felt, would eventually wound me.

I walked him away from the heavy bag and pointed out a few more things which caught my eye. He wrote down prices on a folded sheet of paper. Back at his old desk by the door, he totalled the amount.

I looked at the exorbitant sum. "Does that include delivery?" I asked.

"Delivery?" he questioned, taken aback. "What—you think I'm legit?"

I hesitated. "Maybe I don't need the dining table just yet—or matching chairs."

He looked at me, like the assessor he was, immediately working me out. "See all that stuff back there—all the broken and damaged things?" I nodded. "Well, I need all that stacked up and tossed into a skip I've got coming in two days. Then I need the floor swept."

"Will it include free delivery?"

"You drive a hard bargain, Dougay." He nodded.

"It's a pleasure doing business with you, Remy." We shook hands. I tried to match the strength in his grip. I failed.

Inside three days, his warehouse was neat and tidy and my apartment was sparsely furnished.

*

It was after midnight, and I couldn't sleep. I lay there, looking up, considering what colour I'd one day paint the ceiling. No matter what I thought it could be, I knew I'd decide on white. I always had—I always would. I gave up planning my apartment's decoration. Sleep was eluding me, so I dressed and took myself downstairs to sit in Place Mozart. Maybe the night air could set me off.

There was only one other person down there. He was asleep in a new sleeping bag surrounded by his worldly possessions. I knew the sleeping bag was newly acquired, for I'd given it to him two nights ago, after my furniture had arrived.

Remy must have liked my sweeping style, for he'd tossed in some sheets and a pink duvet, which he claimed had once been rejected by Princess Grace of Monaco. Unfurled on my bed, I could see why she'd rejected it. Lace trim does not suit me.

I sat and stretched my legs forward, tilting back my head to allow the moon to shine on my face. I was literally stargazing, noticing for the first time the constellations above me. Unable to recognise a single cluster, I then nodded, understanding. In Australia, at night, I'd always looked the other way.

A car slowly turned into Rue Beethoven, as if the driver was searching for a street number. It stopped. I heard a door open and then slam shut. The car crawled off, gathering speed. Seated on the bench, I could only make out its top. It didn't appear to be of a cheap make.

I stood and stretched to go back inside, intending to climb the six flights, hoping that the exercise might help tire me. I looked to where the car had stopped. On the footpath was a dark form—a non-geometric shape.

Curiosity aroused, I crossed to it. It was a person. I turned the body over and she moaned, "Don't phone the police. Don't phone the police."

Chapter 2

I managed to get her to her feet. There wasn't much life in her, so she weighed heavily on me. Bending my knees a little, I gave a short upward movement, taking her weight onto my hip. She groaned as our bodies bumped. Together we stumbled to the front door of the foyer.

M'sieur Pom was there, in pyjamas, putting on his glasses. "I heard the car pull up; the slammed door; it driving away." For his age, he had better hearing than me! He came around and helped me hold her. "Who is she?"

"No idea. She didn't fill in my dance card."

"I'll call an ambulance." He left me holding her once again, as he moved hurriedly to his desk.

"No," I countered. "She doesn't want that. No police."

"I'll call the ambulance, not the police," he explained, the receiver in his hand.

"They'll have to report the assault. The police will get involved."

He considered that and hung up. "You can't leave her here—in the foyer."

"Of course not—I'll take her to my room—clean her up."

"What if she dies up there?" he asked. Was my building caretaker a pessimist or a realist?

"If she does then you're the key witness who'll prove my innocence," I said, trying to make light of the severity of the situation. "Open the elevator door, please."

He moved to the back of the foyer and, thinking of the tenants, carefully and quietly slid open the iron door of the elevator. We both gently shuffled her through the door and propped her against the elevator's far wall. She was shaking, unsteady on her feet. I didn't think her condition was drug induced as she didn't have the spaced-out look nor an undernourished appearance of an addict.

Under the door of an adjacent apartment, a light came on. I indicated it to M'sieur Pom. I held onto the young woman while he went to the door and quietly said, "Everything's alright, Madame Legrande. I'm just putting out some late-night rubbish."

Through the door, a quiet muffled reply came back to him. The light went out.

"Ride with the girl, M'sieur Pom," I whispered. "Keep her upright. I'll take the stairs."

On the top floor landing, I gave him my door key and took hold of her, balancing her upright against my shoulder. He opened my apartment door and I stooped and lifted her, as if she were my drunken bride.

"Is this going to be the new norm?" he asked.

"What's that, M'sieur Pom?" I wondered, as I carried her across the threshold.

"You bringing your work home."

*

I carried her to my new second-hand sofa and gently placed her there. I stepped back. "*Merci*, M'sieur Pom. I'll be okay now."

"Yes, but will she?" he asked, with a half-knowing tease in his voice.

"I'm an honourable man, M'sieur Pom."

He smiled and sensed I was. "There's a saying: 'nice guys finish last'," he said.

"I'm not a nice guy," I whispered back.

M'sieur Pom smiled in appreciation of my concern for the young woman, and quietly closed the door behind him.

I had a clean rag, one I hadn't used on the walls, and I held it under the hot water tap in my kitchen. I knelt by her, wiping the dirt from her face. Some of it wasn't dirt—bruising doesn't wipe away on a wet rag. She stirred. I leant back waiting.

She was very attractive, dark-haired and in her mid-twenties. I noticed she had green eyes—the rarest of colours. She didn't ask who I was or where she was. She studied me a moment, didn't recognise me, and then gazed around the room.

"You're poorer than me." She coughed a little. "No police?"

"I haven't called anyone. I'll get you some water."

I did so and held the glass to her mouth. She sipped and coughed again. Her head fell back, and she groaned reaching for her side. I noticed bruising on both sides of her neck.

She was only wearing a dress—one of those whole pieces of cloth that women pull on effortlessly over their head, the shapeless material immediately hugging their figure. And then suddenly, with a pair of sandals on their feet, they're off creating havoc in the lives of men. This young woman looked as if she'd created a lot of havoc, though tonight, sadly, the havoc had been created on her.

She stretched and audibly winced.

"Are you hurt there?" I asked, concerned. "On your side?"

"Both," she managed to say.

"Both sides?"

"Yes." She groaned. As she started to carefully stand, I tried to stop her or help her—I didn't know what I was doing. She held my assistance at bay. "Lift my dress over my head, will you?" I hesitated. "Come on, I can't lift my left arm."

I lifted the plain black dress as requested. She stood there in red underwear—I'd say expensive silk, not that I am an authority on ladies' undergarments.

Down both sides of her body, beginning below the arm pits, were long scratch marks—three on either side. The bottom of the wounds was deeper than the top. Blood had clotted there. Someone with long nails had given her an almighty rip—or some sadistic bastard had done it with a gardening fork. I noted her bra had been put on afterwards—her scars ran underneath the expensive looking material.

"I have some antiseptic cream—I'll get it for you." I went into the bathroom. She followed. She gingerly lifted her right arm above her head and the left to the elbow, away from her body. I searched in the cupboard below the sink.

She leant forward, her right arm extended, taking her balance on the mirror of the vanity above the sink. She studied her face and groaned a little.

I removed her bra. She didn't bat an eyelid. I guess men had undressed her before. I squeezed the cream onto my fingers.

"This will be cold," I warned. I applied the cream carefully. She winced and audibly inhaled as the shock ran through her. She held herself, against the vanity, pushing back until the cold cream warmed.

I went back and found the cloth, wetting it again and wiping dirt from her knees and lower legs. I applied the cream to her scratched knees. Her ankles appeared to have been bound.

I looked up, past the small *fleur-de-lis* tattooed on her right buttock, to the underside of her wrist. They also had been bound.

Finding a warm long-sleeved shirt of mine, I wrapped her in it. I led her back from the bathroom to the sofa. I took the pink duvet from my bed and covered her. She did not smile up at me in appreciation. "Pink," she said. "I'll be safe with you, then."

"Yes, you'll be safe, though not because I sleep under a pink duvet." She'd closed her eyes and was no longer listening. It was as if Father Dougay was bidding his wayward daughter 'goodnight', their estrangement finally resolved. I went to my bed and waited. I heard her breathing settle and take on a regular rhythm. Quietly, I left the apartment and went back down to the foyer.

"She okay?" asked M'sieur Pom. I nodded. "It's been a long time since I've been that close to such a beautiful young woman. Expensive perfume. Where are you going now?"

"I want to see if she's dropped a bag or something outside," I explained.

The old caretaker smiled knowingly at me and held up a purse. He pointed to his head. "Up there for thinking…"

"Did you look inside?"

"Of course. No, do not worry, I did not take anything. Like you, I am an honourable man." I nodded, appreciating his reference to what I'd said earlier. He continued, "Her name is Eloise Pittard. Not much in there—but look at this." He held up a large fold of euro—bound by a money clip. "I counted it—three thousand."

I whistled.

"Who uses a money clip?" the old man asked. I shook my head for I'd never come across anyone who had. He answered his own question with a question. "An American—like in those films?"

"I do not know," I confessed.

M'sieur Pom put the money back into her purse and passed it to me, again asking, "She *is* okay, isn't she?"

"She's asleep—she'll live. She's badly bruised, scratched and she's been bound."

M'sieur Pom thought for a moment. "That explains the amount of cash." I looked blankly at him. "She's been paid to be a punching bag."

My stomach ached. He was right, of course, though I didn't like thinking of that. I hate violence against women and this type of perversion was beginning to appal me. I wasn't going to tell him about the viciousness of the scratches down both sides of her body. She may have been used for a punching bag, however, I felt sure she'd been used for something far worse.

I thanked M'sieur Pom again and took her purse back upstairs and left it on the floor by the sofa. She was sound asleep.

Like Eloise Pittard, sleep no longer eluded me.

When I woke in the morning, she'd gone.

Chapter 3

I still had some of the money Claude had paid me for my three-days scrubbing in his kitchen. I decided to give a small amount of it back to him, as I planned on spending the morning nursing a black coffee at L'Opera Mozart.

It was unceremoniously dumped on the table before me by Marcel, the man I'd been subbing for last week. He was upset about something. I tried engaging him in small talk, however he left my question, "How are you?" dangling, as he returned inside. Perhaps he was simply unfriendly.

After an hour of sitting over my drained cup, I thought I'd head off for a stroll—no place in particular, and if I ended up down by the beach, then a swim. Or better still I could stroll along Promenade des Anglais and admire all the expensive cars I'd never be able to afford. I'd long given up hope of being befriended by any of the women who rode in them.

I found Claude behind the counter and paid him. I suggested, "Why don't you play excerpts from his operas as background music?"

"Whose operas?" he asked, having no idea to whom or what I was referring.

"Mozart's!" I explained.

"Why?" He looked curiously at me.

I pointed to his café's name printed on top of a menu. "Just a thought."

"You Australians are very odd. Listen—you want a job?"

"Marcel planning on being ill again?"

"No. My solicitor was asking around. She needs someone to run messages, deliver papers—but you wouldn't be employed full-time. She only wants someone with time on their hands. I immediately thought of you. Also you seemed reliable when you worked here. You weren't shifty around the cash register." He removed an item from his waistcoat pocket. "That's her card."

*

I stood before a stone building on the opposite side of the Old City in Rue Beaumont. I found the lawyer's name on the directory—third floor. I took the elevator up and turned left. A painted sign on the door read: 'Francine Delange, Solicitor'. I entered.

It was a sparsely furnished office, neat and tidy, with a couple of framed certificates on the wall and a large green pot plant in the corner, next to the window. The slats on the venetian blind were half-opened, splintered light cutting across the room.

The receptionist, not long out of school, looked up eagerly from her laptop. "May I help you?"

"I believe Madame Delange may be looking for me."

"Really?" She commented in disbelief, as if her boss had never looked for anyone. "Whom may I say is calling?"

"Dougay Roberre."

My name meant nothing to her. Why should it? I sat on one of the two waiting chairs. She lifted a handset, put her hand over her mouth and whispered into the receiver. She hung up. "Madame Delange will be with you shortly."

I knew she wouldn't be. I knew I'd be waiting for a while. People who work in these types of offices and in these types of professions seem to believe only *their* time is of importance. I was wrong.

The door to the inner office opened and a tall, sophisticated-looking woman, in a conservative dark grey pantsuit appeared. To add to that striking image, Madame Delange had long jet-black hair that shone, picking up the combined rays of sunlight and overhead lighting. Was the colour natural or not? Who cared? I certainly didn't.

She was removing her reading glasses, a little distracted, as she said, "Monsieur Roberre—please come in."

I eased by her as she held open the door for me, her perfume striking my nostrils, dead centre.

"Please sit," she said, indicating the only chair not on her side of the desk.

I did and I watched her come from the door frame, her torso effortlessly gliding. I assumed she'd had deportment lessons as a teenager. Maybe she'd been a model and thought better of it.

She sat behind her glass and black metallic desk, clasping her hands on it, in front of herself. "Now, what can I do for you?" she asked in a business-like way.

"Claude, from L'Opera Mozart, said you may need a hand."

"A hand?"

"Deliver papers or collect documents for you?"

"Ah—yes." My presence was now making sense to her. She sat forward, business-like. "It is not a permanent position. You'd be called upon as each job arises—and paid accordingly. You have time on your hands?"

"For now," I lied.

She reached for her desk drawer and removed a large envelope. There were two, fifty-euro notes attached to the outside of it by a paper clip. She slid off the money and passed the two notes to me.

"*Merci,*" I said, hoping not to sound overly thankful, as I popped the two notes nonchalantly into my shirt's pocket.

"Take this envelope to the address on it, get it signed where marked and get it back to me by close of trade today. Do not let it out of your sight. The man named there"—she pointed to the envelope—"must sign in your presence. Take this pen with you. Then you sign as witness on the space below his signature. Understand?"

"Yes." I took the documents and pen and left. The receptionist did not look up. Her face was buried in her mobile, no doubt catching up on the exciting lives of her friends and followers.

I looked up the address I needed on my mobile and headed up hill to Cimiez. If I was going to continue delivering documents for Madame Delange, I was going to need to buy a multi-day travel pass for the trams and buses.

After fifteen or so minutes, I checked the address on the envelope against my phone app and stopped walking. I'd found it. The recipient lived in a ground floor apartment, clearly a rental, for in front of it were strewn broken pieces of junk. There was no foyer. Apart from the small cemented entranceway, the front door opened onto the street.

I knocked. The door was opened by a tarty, large bosomed fake blonde who'd seen the best of fifty-five years slip by her. "Yes? What do *you* want?"

"Is Monsieur Lemoine at home?" I asked politely.

"What's it about?" she snarled.

"I need his signature on these papers."

"No, he's not in. Now fuck-off!" She slammed the door shut.

I knocked again. It opened. As she spoke, I put my foot between it and the jam. "Didn't you hear the first time? All you government types are the same. Stupid!" She slammed the door and it immediately rebounded off my foot into her ample chest. She spluttered and staggered back. "You hit me!"

"Stop the carry on and answer the question. Is he inside?"

"No—he's at his office. Unlike you scum, he has a proper job!"

"Address?" She spat out a street name and a number. I left. At the nearest outlet, I bought a multi-day travel pass.

He wasn't at the address. They'd never heard of a 'Monsieur Lemoine'. I was not impressed. I'd now criss-crossed Nice, since leaving L'Opera Mozart this morning, for the better part of three hours. I went back to Cimiez.

The same woman opened the door. Before she could utter any fowl-mouthed invective, I pushed passed her and found Monsieur Lemoine in the kitchen out back. He was wearing a grubby white singlet, which matched the surrounding walls, cigarette in mouth, drinking coffee. He looked up, surprised by my intrusion.

"Sign this please, Monsieur Lemoine," I said, with only a slight trace of annoyance in my voice.

"Fuck off! I'm not signing anything." He stood and came from around the table. "That bitch of a wife thinks she can just take everything." He raised his right fist. "I said: fuck off!"

"And I said: sign!"

He threw the right fist at me. I ducked my head and hit him with a straight left jab to the stomach. He let out a huge "Phooor!"

"I've been wandering all over Nice today looking for you and you've been here all that time, laughing at me behind my back. I'm not a figure of fun!"

"Fuck off!" he shouted, much louder, in case I hadn't heard the first time.

I hit him again, a left jab to the kidneys. He buckled. I handed him the solicitor's pen I had in my top pocket, next to the hundred euro. "You'll be able to sign okay down there on your knees?" I asked with mock concern.

He nodded and groaned. He signed. I took back the documents and pen and was adding my signature when the old tart screamed and jumped onto my back. I dropped my shoulders and flicked her off onto the floor to join her meal ticket. As she hit the floorboards, a water pipe from somewhere inside the apartment shuddered.

"Look," I said, standing over her, showing her the document. "You've ruined half of my signature."

"I'll report you to the government, you bastard!" she screamed looking up at me.

"Go ahead—for the last time—I don't work for the government." I looked down at Lemoine, still clutching his guts. "Piece of advice, Monsieur Lemoine—never lead with your right."

I slammed the door behind me and headed back to Madame Delange's office.

*

"You're back early," said the solicitor, glancing up surprised.

Back early? I thought, settling into the chair opposite her desk. It must have been getting warm in her office for she'd removed her jacket. It had to have been the heat, for she could not have known that I like the look of a black bra beneath a white blouse.

"How long has Monsieur Lemoine been avoiding you?" I asked her, hoping to prolong the conversation with questions, which I had no real desire to hear answered. I was only interested in my eyes being pleasured for as long as possible.

"You're the third delivery I've sent his way."

"Third? What happened to the other two?"

"The first was unable to find him—searched for two days. Though I don't believe he tried all that much. The second returned with a broken nose."

It appeared she had no qualms about me not knowing I'd possibly be given a similar welcome. "Madame Delange, you could have warned me," I said.

"Yes. Forgive me. Sometimes I can overlook minor details."

Minor? I forgave her.

She opened the documents and smiled with relief and pleasure when she read Lemoine's signature. "And you've witnessed it! Thank you. This address you've written here—is it legitimate?"

"Yes." I may not look like an international property owner, for looks can be deceptive. She wasn't deceived.

"Monsieur Roberre—don't tell me in so many words—was there trouble?"

"Not from my point of view, Madame." I rubbed my fist. I think she understood. I rose and began to go.

"Before you go—I was wondering." She dropped her voice. "Are you free Friday evening? No, I'm not asking you on a date. I have to go to a bar I've never been to—birthday drinks with an old girlfriend—and I'm worried about getting home afterwards. To be honest with you, I only drink alcohol on a Friday evening and sometimes my legs get a little wobbly. I don't wish to be taken advantage of in the streets. You understand?" I nodded. "At about 10.30? Could you meet me there and escort me to my apartment, please? Of course, I'll pay you."

"I'll have to cancel that cocktail party at the Monaco Royal Palace," I warned her, "but I'll be there."

Taking back her pen, she wrote down the address of the bar. I folded it into my wallet and hoped I'd left her with the impression that I had royal connections. Intelligent women like her can sometimes be easily fooled. This one wasn't.

Chapter 4

It was closer to eleven than ten-thirty when Francine Delange emerged from the crowded bar. I'd only been waiting on the footpath outside for about thirty minutes. Another fifteen and I'm sure some patrolling policeman would have insisted I move on.

Francine was dressed similarly as before, though the cut of her pantsuit appeared to hug her as if not wanting to let her go. She hadn't lied to me. She was unsteady on her feet. She waved her hand as she recognised me upon emerging from the noisy crowd and stumbled slightly into my arms.

"Thank you," she said, as I caught her. "I'm sorry."

I wasn't, for I rather like having beautiful women fall into my arms.

She straightened herself and in one brief motion, reassembled her clothing. "I do not like the look of inebriated women," she said, her speech slurring slightly. "Walk me home—in the dark, please—in case someone recognises me."

I set off, holding her lightly beneath her elbow. "Where are we walking to?" I asked.

She stopped and thought. She laughed. "About face!" she called out militarily.

We turned 180 degrees and I walked her home. It was a very pleasant evening for a stroll and the further we walked, the more she sobered. From the old city, we headed back to the area of her office, stopping by Place des Cigalusa, Rue Barla to be specific. I hoped I'd remember how to get back the way I'd come, so I could catch a late bus home. When we stood outside her apartment foyer, she'd sobered so much, you'd never have known she'd tasted alcohol at all.

"Hungry?" she asked. "Foolishly, I haven't eaten—possibly why I'm so tipsy. Come on, I'll make us an omelette."

I followed her up the stairs. I still hadn't been paid—that was the reason I followed her, not that she impressed me in any way. Who was I kidding? Francine Delange impressed me a lot.

*

She handed me a bunch of notes—a hundred euro—for the evening stroll home. The woman had money to burn and I didn't object to her kind of fire.

"Tell me your life story in under seven minutes," she asked with humour, as she broke five eggs into a bowl and whipped them into submission. As she turned off the heat of the stove and divided the omelette between two plates, I finished, my life story timed perfectly.

"Australia—fascinating. I should go there one day."

She took a mouthful and we both ate in silence. I wish I knew what she was thinking, what she was weighing up in that silence. I was thinking about how I came to be in her apartment, the circumstances that led me here. And I was thinking of the green eyes of Eloise Pittard. I was hoping her wounds had healed. I was wondering what she was up to right at this very minute. I hoped she wasn't servicing some old depraved man for an enormous amount of money. That's the moralist in me, I'm always—

Francine spoke. "Are you heterosexual or homosexual?"

I was taken aback by the question. "That shouldn't impact upon my future employment," I managed to say. "Nice is a very liberal minded community."

"I'm not asking on behalf of Nice. I'm asking on behalf of myself."

I looked at her. "Heterosexual."

"Are you married? Living with a woman here in Nice? Got your eye on anyone?"

"No—to all three questions." I was wondering to where this line of questioning was leading. Should I be suspicious? She was after all, a lawyer.

She put down her knife and fork and slid her plate away. "I am only prepared to offer you Friday evenings."

"Friday evenings? Like a bodyguard?" Francine Delange eyed me as if she thought I might be leading her on. I wasn't. "I'm sorry, Madame, but I—"

"Call me Francine."

"Francine. I do not follow."

"You're an attractive man, Dougay—rugged, strong-looking. I'd be a couple of years older than you, but I'm still in very good condition. I exercise, I swim. I have not had sex in a very long time."

I nearly choked on the remnants of my omelette. "And you want to have—"

"I'm being adult about it. Here's the offer—only Friday night. You pick me up after client's drinks somewhere in the city—it's always a different bar—and walk me home. The rest of the night is ours. I ask only that you be gone by 7 am Saturday morning. I have things to do."

I took her up on her offer. She hadn't lied. She was still in very good condition.

*

I made my foyer a little after 7 am. I'd left Francine as asked and decided to swim in the sea. Walking back to my apartment, to change and get a towel, I kept going over the prolonged delights of last evening. I knew where I'd be next Friday from 10 pm.

I entered as a little old lady locked her ground floor apartment, the same apartment I'd seen the light come on under the door when Eloise was in the elevator. She walked towards me, dragging her shopping trolley. Her feet got tangled and she lurched forward. I stepped quickly and caught her before she hit the tiles, face first.

"Madame, Madame, are you alright?"

She righted herself. Only then did I release her.

"Monsieur—oh—thank you so much, so much."

I waited while she gathered herself.

"*Merci*—I'm alright now."

Then she smiled at me, with a smile that lit up her face. I could tell, in her youth she'd been a knockout, her blue eyes having lost none of their sparkle. I escorted her through the foyer door and watched her walk away down the street. She didn't go far. A driver emerged from a dark sedan and took her trolley, putting it into the rear. He held the door for her, as she climbed in carefully. She saw me looking after her and waved. I waved back and smiled. The door closed. The car drove off.

I changed upstairs and spent the morning swimming in the public area opposite Rue de Congres. The water here is always of a light green-blue. No doubt a scientist could explain why—I suppose it may have something to do with the type of rock on the ocean floor. Overhead people flew, clutching a parachute being drawn by a noisy speedboat.

I lay on the rocky beach, half-asleep listening to the sounds around me. An occasional Italian or German accent caught my ear, however when I heard a broad Australian accent, I turned over and pretended I was asleep. I nodded off. Clearly, I'd spent more energy last night than I thought I had.

The afternoon I spent at L'Opera Mozart, sipping beer. Marcel was his usual unfriendly self. There was music in the overhead speakers. I pointed this out to Claude.

"Don Giovanni," he informed me, as if it needed no explanation. "Did it work out for you and my solicitor?"

"Marvellously well," I replied.

"Good," he said. He leant into me, "She's an impressive looking woman, isn't she?"

"I didn't notice," I lied. "With me—business is business, Claude."

I ordered another beer and, on my mobile, caught up with the result of the Friday night football game, back in Melbourne. There are some things you can never give up, no matter where in the world you live. They'd be football, beer, and the feeling of a wonderful slightly older female solicitor crawling naked over your prone body in the dark.

Chapter 5

I was sitting on my usual bench in Place Mozart—Sunday evening, rays of sunlight disappearing behind the buildings. I watched my homeless 'friend' enter the small park, dragging his worldly possessions on a two-wheeled cart he'd made a long time ago. He took out the sleeping bag and as he unfolded it onto the ground, he saw me. He came over.

"I see. I see—everything." He pointed to his eye, as if to reinforce, or try to convince me of what he was going to say.

"What do you see, mate?" I asked, prepared to sit and chat with him. I offered him the seat beside me. He didn't take it. He stood a little way from me, shifting his balance from foot to foot.

"You—the other night," he began. "You pick up woman—take her inside."

I sat up straight. "You saw that?" I asked, a sense of urgency in my voice.

"Yes. I saw the car. Y…Y something—or something Y." He stopped. I let him go on. He tapped his head as if trying to shake loose his memory.

He didn't have madness in his eyes, rather a look of disconnection or a bewilderment—a frustration at not being able to get his thought and his expression to come together. I didn't rush him. So much can be forgiven in a person who sleeps every night under the stars and dines on the handouts or scraps of others.

I changed the subject, hoping it may help. "What's your name, mate?" It seemed to work, as he focused on my question.

"Jacques."

I waited for a family name. There wasn't one forthcoming.

"I'm Dougay—pleased to meet you, Jacques." I stood and extended my hand. He looked at it uncomprehendingly. It had been a long time since anyone had offered their hand to him. Shaking it, a smile crossed his face—like a relief, as if he'd been welcomed back into the human race.

"Seven—something," he spurted out. He smiled and nodded, confirming to himself. He was pleased to have remembered.

"Did the 'Y' come before the '7' or vice versa?" I asked.

He held my gaze and angrily hit the side of his head. "No more—can't remember no more."

"Take it easy, don't hurt yourself." I waited for him to calm. "You've done well to remember that. *Merci*, Jacques."

I took out my mobile. I typed into my notes: Y 7. Jacques went back to preparing his bed.

He called back to me, "Good bed. Very warm!"

I waved, "My pleasure." I walked around the corner to L'Opera Mozart.

Claude was doing his final wipe down of the counter. As I came in, he rolled down his shirt sleeves. "You're late, tonight," he commented, doing up the cuffs.

"What food have you got left over, Claude?" I bought two croissants and went back to the park and handed them to Jacques. "*Bon nuit*, mate."

*

I lay in bed, unable to get Francine out of my thoughts. I loved what she'd done to me on Friday night, though I didn't like what she was doing to me now. I was wanting her; thinking of her; feeling the memory of her on me. *It's a Friday night fling—only!* I reasoned with myself. However I rarely listen to self-reason.

Had other women had this effect on me? I couldn't recall. It wasn't just a sexual thing. Francine seemed to be the complete package. I could close my eyes and still hear her voice. And the way she beat those eggs!

I rose and drank a glass of water. I stood in the living area behind the sofa looking onto the deserted street below. Had I made the right decision—tossing in everything in Australia and coming here? Stop it! Stop it! Of course I had. I turned away from the window. That was when I saw, lying on the floor, the shirt Eloise had worn; the shirt I'd wrapped around her near nakedness. It must have fallen from the back of a chair. I'd forgotten all about it. Stooping, I picked it up. I wondered if I could smell her on it. I could. I smiled at my sexist childishness.

There was something in the pocket—a fifty euro note. I wondered out loud, "Why do beautiful women throw cash at me?" I laughed, not believing that for one minute. Though in Francine's case, I hoped it was never going to stop.

I was feeling sentimental. I took the note into the kitchen and pinned it to my small noticeboard—next to my handwritten: *Buy milk!*

*

On Monday morning, a text message from Francine woke me early. It was business. It simply listed a name, an address and a time for later in the day. It contained nothing personal, nothing about how I moved her and nothing about how she couldn't sleep because of me.

The meeting was scheduled for 10.30 am. I had plenty of time. I headed to the sea.

A little before the appointed time, I stood below the office of a private investigator, Jules St Croix, near the Post Office on the narrow Rue Alfred Mortier in Durandy. Up a flight of stairs, his office, immediately off the landing, was shambolic.

The small outer 'office', for want of a better word, was fundamentally a filing cabinet. The private investigator may have believed there was organisation within the room, though I saw no discernible system in place. It was covered in files, all stacked willy-nilly.

"I hope you don't want me to put all those onto a computer for you," I said upon entering. "I don't type."

"We've something in common then." The P.I. was short and squat, in his fifties, with a full head of grey hair and thick matching moustache. "Francine Delange said I could rely on you." He peered closer at me. "Is that true?"

"What did you have in mind?" I asked, avoiding his question. I wanted more information before appearing to commit to a job I knew I wasn't going to refuse.

"Barge into an apartment and keep a dog at bay, while I photograph the fornicating couple."

"Hasn't that kind of stuff gone out of vogue? You don't still need photographic proof to get a divorce, do you? Even Australia's not that backward."

"The wife wants to blacken his name—destroy his standing in society. She's probably got the house and sixty percent of his fortune. Now she wants good old-fashioned revenge. You don't look very interested."

"Well…"

"What? Being Australian makes you too good for the job?"

"No! Anything but!" I retorted.

"Okay, three hundred." He glanced at his wristwatch. "Come on. We don't have a large window of opportunity. He's got this woman over in an apartment in Saint Roch, near the railway line, out of the way, far from prying eyes—though not far enough away from mine."

"How do you know he's over *there*?"

He tapped his nose. "It pays to be connected. She's a high-class hooker and he's some high up public servant—though I didn't tell you that. And you'll forget everything you see and hear while we're over there. Come on—I've a car downstairs."

I wasn't going to need my multi-day travel pass today.

*

Rather than slamming my shoulder to the door, I reached for the handle—surprisingly, it opened. That impressed Jules. Not waiting to tell me so, he barged by me, camera out, clicking. The man looked up, his eyes suddenly widening in surprise. A mass of blonde hair, atop a woman's smooth naked back was giving him a close medical examination of his groin. She didn't leap up. The man didn't scream. The dog leapt up on me and I screamed!

I fell to the floor holding the powerful beast from my throat. My hands were squeezing together around its neck and trying to push upwards at the same time. The dog was not feeling a thing. I don't know what photos Jules managed to take, as all I could see were the ferocious teeth snarling at me in close-up and all I could feel were the droplets of slobber falling onto my face. Suddenly the dog yelped. Jules had kicked it in the side, and I scrambled, following him out the door—job done.

*

Jules offered me a coffee and a bite of lunch downstairs from his office, in a corner café. He studied the camera, nodding in appreciation at the pictures he'd taken. "My client is going to be very happy with these."

"Jules, it's not my business, but what have we really gone and done?"

He looked at me. "Made a living," he replied dismissively. I sipped my coffee and shut my mouth. It was his business—moral questions and all.

He sensed my unease. "A long time ago, I made a decision that I was to be the type of private detective Alexander's mother would never have wanted him to be."

"Alexander?"

"The Great! At his birth, his mother had a choice for him—to live a short glorious life, or a long dull one. She chose the former. I chose the latter. My detective agency has never solved the crime of the century; however, I have managed to stay alive and managed to put food on the table. If you keep putting up your head, someone around here will eventually kick it off. My aim in life is to be old enough to retire."

He took three hundred euro out of his inside coat pocket and handed it to me. He fiddled with his camera. After a while, he said, "Look—I admit—the wife's probably a bitch. And she needs the cards turned on her. From what I hear, she's no moralistic beacon of female virtuousness. Word is she's supposed to be fucking some guy. In fact, word is, she'll fuck anybody." He looked carefully at me. "If you want redemption—then I could take photos of 'you' screwing 'her'!"

"No way! You screw her—I'll take the photos!"

Jules shivered at the thought. He passed the camera to me.

"This is what money buys you. Imagine having an hour with her in your bed. This blonde has got a great ass, my friend."

He tapped the camera. I scrolled through the photos he'd taken that morning. He was right—a great ass, with a tattoo of a *fleur-de-lis* upon it.

Chapter 6

Nothing happened for the next two days in regard to my employment. Claude didn't need help in the kitchen; Jules wasn't bursting through any doors; and Francine didn't text, 'Dougay, how are you coping without me?'

However something important did happen, which would reverberate positively for me going forward.

I was sitting in Place Mozart with Madame Legrande, the little old lady from the apartment on the ground floor, back near the elevator. The sun was high in the sky and she'd invited me over to join her on *her* favourite bench. I was glad of the company. I sat there listening to her stories.

In her younger years, she'd been a beach beauty queen. She said that she'd been snapped in the sand at Cannes Festival time, modelling a bikini, the photograph being published in an American newspaper. And this I felt was the highlight of her memoirs—she'd managed to get so close to Yves Montand, she actually kissed him!

It was of a world and a time long gone. All I could tell her in return were tales of me surfing waves; Sunday afternoon barbeques with mates; and a woman who broke up with me and went off and married another man.

"Marriage!" She sat back and reflected. "It's funny, isn't it? I married a wealthy man, you know. I never wanted for a thing. I had an unlimited credit card; a once-a-year-holiday of my choosing; and he gave me two sons who adore me and though they are very different, I adore them. My husband was very generous to me—financially. Of course, there was a catch. In return for all that, I had to employ a blind eye when it came to his—'extra-curricular activities'. I was never allowed to question how he made his *real* money. But I knew one thing—he had to have other women." She turned to me. "Why is that?"

What could I possibly say? It's unsettling to have an elderly lady tell you intimate details of a past life she now had doubts about. Or perhaps she was now of an age, and a reconciled mind-set, where those doubts no longer worried her.

She held her chest and slumped back on the bench. I phoned for an ambulance. I rode in the back with her, holding her hand, to the hospital. I followed her on the stretcher and after the nurses 'wired' her in, I sat by her bed until two men appeared. A well-dressed man was accompanied by a very large man.

I excused myself, as I stood to go.

"Who are you?" the well-dressed, smaller man asked.

"A neighbour, a friend. We were just sitting in the park together…"

"Are you the man who also stopped my mother from falling the other day?"

"Yes."

"What's your name, Monsieur?"

"Dougay Roberre." He reached for his wallet. "No, monsieur, no. There is no price on kindness." I bid them *adieu*. I waved to Madame Legrande lying there in her bed. She smiled back meekly. The well-dressed man noted his mother's response.

"Monsieur, if you wait, I'll give you a ride home." The well-dressed man was persistent. "It is the least I can do."

"No need, thank you, monsieur," I said. "I have a multi-day travel pass."

I left the room. Outside in the corridor sat a similar looking man. It was as if he was waiting his turn to be alone with her. He had a distinct quality about him. *Un flic,* I thought, as I walked by. In Sydney, Nice, anywhere in the world, cops all have the same aura.

*

"Have you ever heard of the American film producer Harold Kempenski?"

I was sitting in Francine's office, pleased she'd called. Even though it wasn't Friday night, I was happy to see her. I'd have preferred seeing her standing before me slowly untying her jet-black hair…I snapped out of it. "Francine, I don't go to the movies much."

"It doesn't matter." With her fingers, she flippantly flicked away my ignorance. "He's in town again. He's always here—every summer. He has a yacht moored in Cannes."

"Can I get there on my multi-day travel pass?" I asked jokingly.

She picked up on it, however in her office, business is business. "Claim a return train fare. Make sure you bring me the receipt."

She went on though I wasn't really listening. I was thinking of last Friday evening. She read my mind. Dropping her voice, she said, "I deliberately will not mix business with pleasure. Pleasure is the time from Friday 10.30 until 7 the next morning. Business is everything else. Now concentrate."

It was the sweetest reprimand I'd ever had.

"Go to this address in Nice and wait until this screenwriter—Philip J. Phillips—gives you a completed screenplay. You then take it immediately to Kempenski's boat—*The Blue Dahlia*. It's moored in the marina in Cannes. I've drawn a diagram for you."

She passed me a piece of paper with lines on it. I studied it. I was thankful she'd written over a large area of it 'Mediterranean'. I now had a reference point for her meaningless squiggle.

"If that's all it requires, can't a courier do it?" I asked.

"You stick with this writer until he's finished writing it, even if it takes a day, a week. If needs be—you sleep there; you eat there. Understand?"

"Babysitting as well, huh?"

She ignored my snide comment. "Mister Kempenski is a client. I do the occasional legal work for him when he's here in France. He arranges investment in French film. I promised I'd put my *best* assistant on it."

I raised my eyebrows at that. She looked me in the eye. "I, too, can use conversational humour."

I nodded, conceding my position in the relationship. We were only ever going to be equals in her bedroom on Friday evenings.

"His production assistant, Ms Walton, will read the relevant changes and only then if Kempenski is satisfied, the job is concluded. If he's not satisfied, you take the screenplay back to the writer's apartment in Nice, and he begins the adjustments. Got that?" I nodded. "Here—all the addresses." She handed me a second piece of paper. This one made sense. I held her hand a little. "Stop that," she said unconvincingly. She didn't remove her hand. I played with her fingers.

"And if the rewrites are lousy and I'm still waiting for a finished product by 10.30 on Friday evening?" I asked suggestively.

"Then we both miss out," she said, inhibiting my forwardness.

"I'd better get on to it then," I said, accepting harsh reality and not wishing to waste a second. I headed for the door.

Her voice stopped me. "If you're not back by 10.30 on Friday evening, we could meet on Sunday afternoon at Villefranche-sur-Mer for a swim—if you like."

That took me by surprise. An image of her emerging from the sea and running into my arms didn't linger. Her voice cut it short.

"What are you waiting for?" she asked. "Go to Cannes," she ordered.

At the door I turned. "If this screenwriter is good at his craft, and delivers before Friday's deadline, is there any chance of both?" She said nothing. "Friday night *and* Sunday afternoon?"

She smiled enigmatically and waved me goodbye.

*

Philip J. Phillips was holed up in a luxurious apartment overlooking the sea, one block from Promenade des Anglais, down the end near to where that infamous truck had ploughed into all those innocent people. No writer could afford to be living in this luxury, on the Riviera, this close to the Mediterranean. The Hollywood producer must be paying.

A beautiful blonde woman opened the door. No writer could afford the company of such a stunning companion. The Hollywood producer was definitely paying.

"Hi! I'm here to collect a screenplay," I said, a little too exuberantly, as I was taken by the vision in front of me.

The young woman shrugged—she had no idea what I was talking about.

"I've got the correct place, haven't I? Philip J. Phillips?"

"Yes," she said, unconcerned. "I think that's his name."

She pushed by me. She was off to the beach to lie in the sun, to swim a little and to turn heads a lot. Once she left, I wondered if she was the blonde in Jules' camera. 'There are many blondes in Nice,' I told myself, attempting to dismiss the thought, however, I kept wondering. She could have been. She had all the prerequisites.

I sat, unattended and waited.

It was an impressive apartment. The kitchen seemed to have all top of the range appliances—double-fronted stainless-steel fridge; double fan-forced oven; induction cook top; double sink with vegetable wastage; built-in microwave; and a dark grey marble stone-clad island bench. I was really impressed when I noticed it had a small standalone wine and beer fridge. It was the exact opposite of my kitchen back at Avenue Auber. What did it take to own a place like this? Ah well, one day…

I stood by the balcony door overlooking the Mediterranean. A while later, I sat on the very comfortable sofa.

In the old days I guess I'd have heard from deeper in the apartment, the writer banging away on his typewriter. However, these days, with computer keyboards, it was hard to tell if the writer was working or sleeping. My thoughts happily returned to the blonde. I closed my eyes, put back my head and luxuriated in them.

I jumped with a start when the writer spoke, standing over me. In halting and poorly accented French, he said, "One hour—I finish. Make coffee." He left me to it.

I found the coffee maker hiding in a cupboard. Two cups of coffee later, I needed the bathroom. He re-emerged from his room and took a hat from the stand by the entranceway. "Where are you going?" I asked in English, alarmed. He did not have the screenplay under his arm!

He stopped for a moment. "You speak English? Where'd you learn it? New Zealand?"

"Australia."

"Mmm. I need to walk. I think better when I walk." He left. I zipped up my jeans and followed, letting the door slam behind me. I hoped he had a key!

We walked together on the promenade. I was half a step behind him, saying to myself, "Come on mate—think, think, think—get this masterpiece finished!" I could see my night with Francine disappearing, lost in the fog of his writer's block. He stopped at the large stone steps leading down onto the beach. People pushed passed us—up and down.

We leant there looking over the people below. He was thinking 'plot'—I was admiring 'scenery'. I looked at the beach, convincing myself I had an honourable reason to be doing so. I was looking for his blonde, making sure she didn't get into any difficulty while swimming somewhere out there in the turquoise blue. I delude myself quite often.

"Do you go the movies?" he asked seriously, turning to me.

"Not a lot." My lack of enthusiasm didn't faze him.

"What's your favourite film?" he asked, as if it carried importance.

"Me? I can't really say."

"A great help," he said dismissively.

"I've never thought about it—never had to."

He sighed in frustrated acceptance. He needed someone to bounce ideas off. He'd looked at me as if I was capable of doing that. For him, I guess, I was better than talking to a wall back in the apartment. He went on.

"I'm stuck—the ending. Oh, I've got the villain dead and the hero with the smoking gun in his hand looking over him, but I want—I need—a line to go out on—something memorable to close out the story."

I don't know why or how, but sometimes things just pop into my brain. I said, "*Au revoir,* mate!"

He looked at me, quite taken. He lifted his hand from the stone wall and pointed it down in front of himself. He made the shape of a gun. He pulled the 'trigger'. He lifted the 'barrel' to his lips and blew across the end of it. He tilted back the rim of his imaginary hat with it. He looked back down to the ground and said, "*Au revoir*, mate! Fade to black."

Chapter 7

Cannes smells of money. Beautiful people parade; rich people drive open-top sports cars; poor tourists put on a clean shirt to walk around the place. Under that kind of pressure, I thought I'd better spruce myself up a little.

I made a deviation on my way from Phillips' apartment to Gare de Nice. I had to rummage a bit through my non-extensive wardrobe. Mixing and matching, I found a combo I felt I'd not be embarrassed to wear. I even shaved.

On a dock with Francine's map in my hand, I tried to fathom out which line of tightly packed yachts I needed to walk between. I tried to imagine the collected worth of the marina. I gave up—huge amounts of money are beyond my comprehension.

I had the completed screenplay under my arm and I was wearing a clean dark blue polo shirt over cream trousers. I wore a Panama hat on my head, the band of which read: *Bondi Icebergs*. Would I ever go back there and swim with the old men in the winter sea? Probably not.

I walked down the pier I thought Francine's scribble indicated. A woman's voice asked, "Is that my screenplay?"

I looked at the name on the rear of the moored boat: *The Blue Dahlia*. I said that it was.

"Come aboard." I stepped gingerly up the short gang plank. A lot of accidents happen on boats and I didn't want to spear myself on a railing. I needed to be a hundred percent operable for Friday night.

She held out her hand, waiting for the script. She had the aura of a 'no prisoners taken' type woman. She was my age, perhaps a little older, and not unattractive.

She wore no makeup. The few facial lines and crow's feet were not cemented in—her face had character. I immediately had the feeling that she couldn't have cared less what I or anyone else thought of her. Her auburn hair was pulled back in a pony tail, away from her face, probably whipped there this morning upon rising. A light blue pullover, branded with the yacht's name over her substantial left breast, was pulled well down over dark blue jeans. No nonsense dressing for a no-nonsense woman. I figured, 'To have her as a mistress, you'd need to sign away your life before the first kiss.'

"I have to deliver this to a…" I consulted my note.

"Ms Walton. That's me. Now hand it over," she commanded. I gave her the screenplay. "Sit there. I'll read this and return." She looked up onto the deck above. "Matty?" She waited a moment. There was no movement from above. "Matty!" she called louder and sharper. "A drink for the courier!" she said in unaccented English. She went inside—I presumed down where the cabins were.

A fit seaman, wearing a pale blue polo shirt, similarly labelled as Ms Walton's, climbed down the narrow ladder. He worked out. He saw me and knew my type, because I was his type—a fellow man-for-hire. The difference was he had a permanent job and I was definitely casual.

Above came the raucous explosion of exuberant male laughter. A woman's bare legs crossed from one side of the deck to the other. I caught the sight of a red silk G-string. A *fleur-de-lis* was tattooed on her right buttock. *Eloise?* I wondered. She disappeared from view. *No*, I reasoned. *She'd still be mending her bruises—in private, not public.*

Matty placed a tall glass in my hand. I sipped iced tap water. No alcohol—no wonder rich people stay rich. He stood by the stern and looked out over the tightly packed marina. Another man, older, trimmed grey beard, and dressed similarly, came down the steps and joined him out there. They didn't touch, though I sensed immediately they were in a relationship. Their bodies were too familiar with each other—even standing apart.

I tilted my head back, closing my eyes. I wasn't trying to sleep, rather putting my brain into neutral to help me through what could be a long wait. Above I heard a shuffle of feet. I opened them.

A beautiful woman came down the stairs and went into the galley. She was wearing a high cut black one piece with a short white man's shirt over the top. Her hair was tied up under a multi-coloured scarf. She returned with a glass of blue liquid. I'd recognised her the moment her head straightened, after dipping below the decking above, having instinctively smiled as if we were old friends, though she didn't return the smile. We weren't old friends.

I'd seen her in things—films, half watched on television; magazine covers glanced over while waiting for the dentist. I couldn't put a name to the face. However, when she climbed back up and I studied her ass, it came to me. I realise that sounds sexist—however it was true. She'd always worn tight fitting leather in her action films and I loved whenever she ran away from the camera. I guess it was in the brief given to film directors to make a feature of her natural acting talent. I'd recognised Belinda Swann.

Matty removed the empty glass from my hand. His older lover passed, and said in halting, heavily French accented English, "I must—go—to bridge."

Matty smiled back and took my empty glass to the galley. He returned and stood once again on the stern, as if keeping an eye on me, in case I ran off with the twenty-four-carat gold anchor. I played with my hat, turning its rim, circling it through the fingers of one hand.

Then my eyeballs fell out of their sockets. The G-stringed woman from up on deck came down. I should have kept staring, however the gentleman in me looked away—not for long, though. My blood started to boil—Matty's went ice cold. Before she disappeared into the galley, I did manage to reconfirm that she had the same sized tattoo on her as Eloise.

This woman was a redhead—though I couldn't say if she was a natural, for there was nothing to check that against. She didn't have a single hair on her body. Over her red G-string she wore a pale white blouse, the buttons of which were done up incorrectly. I wanted to re-button them for her. I do like symmetry when it comes to see-through blouses.

When she returned to climb back up on deck, she handed my eyeballs the most serenely prolonged experience. I thought, *Dark-haired Eloise; the blonde in the camera; and now this redhead. Someone had put together a very attractive set.*

I tilted my head back and thought of seriously trying to nod off this time, while I waited for Ms Walton to evaluate the screenplay. I closed my eyes and heard steps on the ladder. I opened them. A man in his early thirties climbed down. He was muscled and oiled, wearing tight brief swimming trunks with a package that demanded attention. He went into the galley and reappeared with two opened bottles of beer. Rather than take them up onto deck, he went by me, deliberately not noticing, and stopped before Matty.

"Care for one?" he asked in English. He was American, with an accent I couldn't place. Maybe he'd spent a childhood moving between states.

"No, sir—Mister Andrews—I never drink on duty," Matty replied respectfully.

"Call me Beau."

"I'm sorry—Beau—not when I'm working."

The American turned to go, thinking better of it. "Tonight, after the skipper has retired, you feel like a late-night fuck?" I tried not to react. Matty looked past the American to me. My eyes were staring blankly ahead. I was giving nothing away. I kept spinning my hat.

The American turned and looked at me. "A delivery boy—who speaks English? I think not!" He turned back to Matty. "So? You interested in my offer?"

"I'm sorry, Beau, but I'm in a long-term relationship with Skipper. I'd never jeopardise that."

"I'd be prepared to reward you," persisted Beau. "In my experience, money buys many favours and people will do many things to get their hands on it."

"I'm sorry, Beau."

"A pity. I've never had a similarly buffed man as me. Maybe on shore? In a couple of days? I know a quiet place—a place where we can make as much noise as possible—a basement—really enjoy ourselves. I'd let you hit me. You'd like that? I know I would. Or would you rather I hit you? All to the body—no facial wounds—we don't need others to figure out what we've been up to. Make for a great souvenir of my time here on the Riviera."

Matty smiled and said respectfully, more than the American deserved, "I love Skipper, Beau."

A deflated Beau walked past me and derogatorily spat, "What's it like being a loser?" I didn't react. He called out up the ladder, "Cal! Care for a beer?" He went up, carrying the two bottles. Matty found a rope to coil. I spun my hat.

Above, on deck, the occasional motion criss-crossed through the opening at the top of the ladder as people changed positions in the sun. I saw a man I hadn't noticed before take hold of the redhead and grip her ass tight into his groin. She didn't object. She started fiddling with him. I needed to drift off—it was all getting too hot for me to bear.

Ms Walton returned. She ignored me. She called to the upper deck, without looking up. "Mister Kempenski? The screenplay is here." She'd spoken English again, with a posh sounding accent, though to my ear it could have been false.

I heard a deck chair scrape and an audible groan as a heavy man rose to his feet. The international producer, Harold Kempenski, appeared on the top of the steps. He bent forward. "And?"

"Nearly. Not quite."

"Send it back!" came the belligerent, shouted reply. "Tell Phillips he's got another twenty-four hours."

My heart sank. Ms Walton handed me the manuscript. Returning to French, she said, "I've marked what Phillips needs to alter."

I retraced my steps between the billions of euros floating on the water and glanced cursorily at the manuscript. Ms Walton's red scrawl seemed to be all over the thing. I was never getting to Francine's at this rate.

Up on street level, I stopped and pretended to take my bearings. A uniformed man, cap in hand stood by the car he was chauffeuring. The car hadn't taken my eye, however its plate had—YKE-738.

I smiled and walked over. "Excuse me sir, but I was wondering."

"In English, please?" he asked with a heavy eastern European accent.

"Excuse me, mate. I'm over here from Australia, and I used to do a bit of driving back home. Is there much work available for this kind of thing—you know, chauffeuring? I'm starting to run out of money. The Riviera's not cheap."

He looked me up and down. "You need to do training."

"I know how to drive—I used to chauffeur back in Sydney," I lied.

"No. You have to study—streets, places, museums, you know."

I have many odd theories regarding life; how to live; and how to deal with the people in it. One of them is that if you want to find out things, always appear to be dumber than the person you need the information from. That way they feel superior and let their guard down.

"Who do you work for?" I asked. No reply. "Do you know if they need other drivers?"

He didn't move. He was assessing the kind of driver I was. Or the kind of financially desperate tourist I hoped I appeared to be. He opened the car door and reached for the glove box. He handed me a business card. I didn't look at it, rather I waved it back to him as I turned happily away. I stopped. "Where you from?"

"Czech Republic."

"Ah," I replied. "Czech beer—the best in the world."

For the first time during our brief meeting, he smiled. Another odd theory of mine is, if you ever want to get anyone on side, tell them their beer is the best in the world. However, be warned, that won't work on the English!

I walked briskly to the station. I read the card on the train—'Riviera Limousines'. There followed a phone number and web address. They were based in Nice. He hadn't been standing in front of a stretch limousine, one of those elongated hearses for the living, though nonetheless it was an expensive looking vehicle. And it was a dark navy blue—almost black in colour.

I held the precious manuscript to my chest wondering how long it was going to take that writer holed up in the apartment overlooking the sea, to get it finished to Ms Walton's satisfaction. If the blonde was back from swimming, it was going to take him a long time.

I thought of the brush with fame I'd just experienced. I took out my phone and read about Belinda Swann. Turns out she's married to occasional co-star Calvin deMarko. I didn't know that. Apparently, they'd been high-school sweethearts. I didn't know that either. Their last film together, *Gothila's Revenge*, was the highest grossing film of last year, displacing their previous film together, *Gothila*. I knew absolutely none of that. I hadn't seen either film. 'That's twenty euro the films didn't gross,' I joked to myself.

I searched and read about Philip J. Phillips. Seems he's an Academy award nominee. Twice married and divorced, he'd had a famous—scandalous—affair with an actress I'd never heard of. Then again, all those Hollywood affairs are 'scandalous', and as I'd never heard of her, I'm sure she'd never heard of me.

*

I handed Philip J. Phillips his edited masterpiece. He glanced at the red comments liberally scattered throughout. "Fuck!" was all he said. He held open the final page. "The only thing that bitch seems to have liked is the last line. *Your* last line!" He laughed; his anger short lived. "Can you cook?" he asked.

"Yes."

"Rustle us up some grits, will ya?" he requested with a false cowboy accent. He went into his room. The blonde came out pulling on one of his shirts over her red silk knickers. Phillips was planning on writing!

In the small kitchen area, the blonde squeezed by me. It seemed today I was destined to be in close contact with semi-naked adorable women. I knew come tomorrow, the joys of today would be gone. She opened the small bar fridge and began making herself a large Bloody Mary.

"Would you like one?" she asked.

"Sure!"

She stirred both glasses and we clinked, before she sat on the sofa, her legs up under herself.

As I searched the fridge for food to cook, she said, "I'm a vegetarian."

"Then I won't go outside and shoot the first cow I see wandering up Promenade des Anglais." She looked at me as if I was a first-class dumb-wit. She'd not understood my humour. She wasn't the first woman not to.

She sipped her drink, sitting there in all her glorious beauty, sexuality and desirability.

During the course of the evening, after we'd eaten the dish, I'd prepared by copying Francine's egg whipping skills, and Phillips went back to his writing, she lay about in the living room, playing with her mobile, endlessly flicking through social media. I came to believe that she was, very possibly, the blonde in Jules' camera. It was confirmed when Philip J. Phillips called her to bed and I caught a glimpse of her tattooed ass, as she rose from the sofa. Yes, someone had put together a first-class trio.

I slept the night on the couch. After some time in the dark, I heard the writer let out a scream of joy. I hoped he'd finally finished the screenplay and not merely achieved satisfaction at the hands of his purchased blonde.

I woke and stretched, thinking I would never get the aches out of my bones. I thought of Eloise and thought of her sleeping, painfully cramped on my old sofa. I knew why she'd left early. If I hadn't had to return his manuscript to Cannes, I'd have left early as well—right after the blonde had said, "This omelette's not very nice."

*

I was back waiting aboard *The Blue Dahlia*. It was midmorning—Friday. I was hoping there'd be no more re-writes required. I was itching to find Francine in whatever bar in town she'd be drinking in and walk her home in the shadows, my arm around her, holding her upright.

I'd brought the manuscript back yesterday and had been sent away with it a second time. Philip J. Phillips had sworn again, however to his credit, he knuckled down and banged on his laptop all night, only stopping to eat a steak I cooked for him. To make it palatable, I covered it with every condiment I could find in the well-stocked kitchen.

The blonde wasn't there, so the meal was free of culinary criticism. Maybe she had to work as well. I never saw her again. For a woman who'd made such a lasting impression on me, I didn't even know her name. If Kempenski agreed to this re-write, I'd never see Philip J. Phillips again, either. As he walked back to his room to recommence writing, I asked, "Any chance of a credit for that final line?"

"Hell no!" he shouted back.

*

Ms Walton stood before me, dressed similarly as the previous three days, though for the first time she wore dress shorts. She had nice legs. I was clearly missing Francine.

Ms Walton turned up her nose at me. "Is that a uniform?" she asked, taking in my crumpled state. "If it is, perhaps you could ask them for a second one." I'd been in my best blue and cream clothes for well over two days—day and night. I guess my body odour had lost its freshness.

Once again, she called up to Mister Kempenski on deck. "And?" he shouted back.

"I think you'll approve."

I sighed a huge relief. Harold Kempenski came down. It was the first I'd really seen of him. He was nuggetty, bare-chested, and had the presence of a street fighter. Matty, at the base of the steps, moved to one side to let him pass. He took the manuscript from Ms Walton and perused the last few pages, merely flicking them over. He called back up the steps. "Cal? Cal!" The American actor Calvin deMarko appeared at the top of the ladder. "You'll love it. I'll have your signature by nightfall."

Beau rushed down. "I'll take it up for Cal, Mister Kempenski." The producer gave it to him and back up he went.

Kempenski said to Ms Walton, "That guy will do anything to please his boss—a real cock-sucker and ass-licker." She looked at me. I was in my French only mode, giving nothing away, though I wondered if Kempenski knew how literally correct he'd been.

The producer looked at his gold wristwatch, which was probably worth the value of my kitchen, and said, "Mary-Anne, take the rest of the day off." He climbed unsteadily up the ladder.

Ms Walton turned to me and in French said, "That will be all. Tell Madame Delange the cheque's in the mail."

Kempenski reappeared at the top of the ladder and whistled at me. I looked up. "Here!" he shouted. "Twenty euro for the delivery boy!" He made a point of dropping the crumpled note away from me. I bent, reached and picked it up. I was not impressed with being treated as a serf.

*

The driver was up on street level again, standing by his car. As I approached, I waved. He tossed a half-finished cigarette onto the ground and stood on it, as if I'd caught him smoking behind the toilet block at school.

"You call the management?" he asked.

"Not yet—too busy. I've been babysitting a writer and delivering and redelivering a script to those Hollywood people down there. I'll call early next week." When you're really interested in following up on a lead, it is best not to express too much interest.

"Like in Sydney, eh?" I asked him. He didn't follow. "You spend a lot of time waiting around, not driving."

"Oh, this job is good," he said. "Special hire." He leant into me. "Like you—American movie stars."

I nodded in approval, making out I was impressed. "Big tippers?"

"The best." He smiled and nodded knowingly. I waved and walked off.

On the train, I searched my phone for the location of a Czech bar in Nice. There was only one—Vlatava-Elbe.

A text message pinged. It was from Francine. She'd sent me the name of the bar she'd be at tonight. I sent a text back, 'OK'.

Smiling, I happily put my mobile back into my pocket. I leant back in my seat, hoping that the train back to Nice would not run off the rails.

Chapter 8

On Saturday afternoon, after smiling and waving at the CCTV camera, I banged on the roller door at Remy's warehouse. He opened the single steel one.

"So!" he said greeting me, a half-smile of pleasure emerging on his face. "You've come to have the stuffing knocked out of you?"

I ignored his excuse for wit and entered. We crossed to the area over by the heavy punching bag. True to his word, he had sweat gear waiting there for me, though mauve is not my most flattering colour.

"This looks new." I inspected the clothing closer. There was a red stain on the chest of the sweatshirt.

"Not new," corrected Remy. "The previous owner bled a little. Hope you don't."

I smelt the stain. "This is tomato ketchup!" I turned back to him. Remy roared with laughter.

We danced about each other for a while, miming blows. He held up his hand to stop me. "Had enough, old man?" I asked cockily.

He didn't comment on that, saying, "Every time, before you lead with your left, you move your head to that side. You're predictable—you're telegraphing your punches. Try throwing a straight left and either keeping your head still or moving it slightly to the right."

I did. We sparred on, more dancing and avoidance than actual contact.

"Okay," he said, beginning to breathe heavily. "I'll stand—you do rapid combinations into my hands—like this—watch!"

He demonstrated. He feigned a rapid left-right-left. He stopped and looked to see if I understood. Perhaps I gave the impression that I hadn't, for he mimed another left-right-left combination as fast as the first. "I call this the Remy Didion Special!" He laughed while gasping for breath. "Now, your turn!"

I threw left—right—left combinations at him until I grew weary.

"Okay, dance," he commanded, without any sense of savage authority in his voice. We bobbed and weaved, bouncing on the balls of our feet.

"Okay," he finally conceded. "That'll do."

I dropped my fists. He hit me with a straight left to the right side of my chest which spun me.

"What'd you do that for?" I said in aching surprise. "I thought you said we'd finished!"

"Never trust an opponent."

*

On Sunday, after a bite of cheese and breadstick, I took the train two stops east, emerging from the tunnel at Villefranche-sur-Mer. I followed the troop of day trippers, under the railway line, out of the exit and down the path to the water. Today the sun was lighting the Mediterranean in all its finest postcard beauty.

I dodged slow moving cars trying to find somewhere to park and slowly walked along the narrow footpath, side-stepping passers-by, past all the already tightly parked vehicles, glancing down towards the water on my right.

Francine was down there—on the sand—I couldn't believe it—beneath a small beach umbrella, tanning her legs.

I was surprised that I had found her so easily amongst the crowded activity of families and friends. A beautiful woman, alone, lying on the sand—maybe I have a natural radar for these things!

We spent about three hours—swimming, drying each other, lying in the sun. I was a very happy man. We walked back toward the train station. I carried her beach paraphernalia. Leaving the sand, a beach ball bounced off my head. I ignored it. Had I finally found Heaven on Earth?

She bought me a cold beer in a bar wedged beneath the cliff. I *had* found Heaven on Earth!

We climbed the hill to the train. She didn't take me back to her place. She got off the train one stop later, virtually after it had poked its head out of the western side of the tunnel. I tried to follow her, however she simply said, "No." She did deign however to turn and wave an off-handed goodbye from the platform.

The sense of Heaven on Earth can be fleeting.

*

"Right. You're here. Let's go!"

Remy had called, asking me to come over. He needed a second pair of hands to help pick up some furniture.

"Where's the guy who usually helps you? You didn't fill your warehouse by yourself." We were in his old white truck heading to the area around Eglise Sainte-Jeanne d'Arc.

"He's gone and shacked up with his brother's wife," said Remy. "I'm a moral kind of guy. I lost all respect for him after that. I had to let him go." I didn't know whether to believe him or not. Remy noted me thinking on what he'd said. He laughed.

"Why didn't you just say you fired him?" I asked, not particularly pleased with his verbal run-around.

"Where's the entertainment value in that?" I had no answer—he was right. "I'm a fighter—a showman to the end!" he exclaimed joyously. Remy was a man who clearly enjoyed his work.

He drove and I drifted into the memory of the weekend. It was Wednesday; however I hadn't got over it yet. I'd decided Francine was two women in one. There was the lawyer and there was the lover. There could not have been a greater contrast. I recalled last Saturday morning lacing up my shoes, sitting on the edge of her bed, when I had asked, "Tomorrow afternoon at the beach? Is that still happening?"

"Maybe," she had replied, accompanied by that wonderful enigmatic look she achieved by simply raising her eyebrows.

Well, as you know, 'maybe' became 'definitely'. However, in the following two days, she'd kept me on edge thinking of her, and even after spending time together that Sunday afternoon on the sand and in the water, I was no further down the track with her than when I first agreed to escort her home.

Remy stopped out the front of a nondescript apartment block. "Stay there," he said, as if I was a faithful hound. After several minutes he returned and drove the truck on further, then turned and came to the rear of the building.

We were met by a man I wouldn't consider buying a used car from. Remy introduced us, "Serge—Dougay; Dougay—Serge." He grunted at us both and I followed him, as Remy slowly drove the truck down a concrete drive to the basement below.

Serge manually rolled up the metal door and Remy manoeuvred his truck back and forth, and finally reversed towards it. Serge shouted, holding up his hand, "Keep the truck outside. I've just finished cleaning up in there!"

The first thing that struck me was the potent smell of disinfectant. The caretaker turned on the overhead garish fluorescent strip lighting. The concrete floor had been hosed, several puddles remaining. He pointed to the far corner to the few pieces of furniture stacked there. He needn't have bothered—we couldn't have missed them—they were the only pieces in the space.

In the opposite corner was a shower. The corners of the two walls were tiled with large quality cream, trimmed with a single line of maroon. I liked the idea of the maroon trim. Maybe I'll do something like that when I get around to renovating my bathroom. It looked incongruous, stuck there in an otherwise barren space. In the corner behind me was a doorway in a crudely painted wall, a kind of makeshift office. I guessed the toilet was in there.

As I crossed, I noticed switches on the wall. They weren't the normal kind you find in your home. These switches were capable of taking a heavy load of electricity. It was as if no one had yet divided the space and constructed rentable studios.

Remy handed me a shifting spanner and I began taking the frame of the iron bed apart. Once I'd done that, Remy lead the way as we carried the heavy pieces to the truck. We walked back for the mattress. *Yes*, I thought to myself, *I'll be using a maroon trim*.

I bent to heave up the mattress. Remy looked with mock askance when the thing slipped out of my fingers. "Never carried a mattress?"

I said nothing. Over the past few meetings I'd managed to play his 'apprentice' to perfection.

"Take hold of it by the side handles," he said, as if speaking to his young son. I did so and we heaved it up onto the dismantled frame. I rolled the carpet and tied it with a thin string, the only one at hand. As we lifted it onto the top of the mattress, the string gave way. There was a dark stain on the otherwise perfect rug.

"Turn that over," said Remy. "Cover it and tie it down. There's a tarpaulin and rope under the front seat—your side. Bind it all together. I don't want it sliding about in there."

I did so, while Remy went and talked with the caretaker. He received a handful of cash. As they spoke their final words, I lifted the edge of the mattress, curiously wishing to see its underside. It had a similar stain, though someone had tried to wash it clean. I tied the load.

Back in the truck, heading towards Remy's warehouse, I said, "Good luck getting that carpet cleaned before you resell it."

"I'll be burning it—and the mattress. I want you to pull it apart when we get back. The springs might come in handy. Burn all the stuffing."

He backed the truck into his warehouse and locked the roller door behind it.

"Tomorrow we're going back. I've talked Serge into buying one of the beds out back for replacement. Afternoon will do—I know how difficult it is for you young active fellows to rise early."

*

Before 9 am, I was sipping my morning coffee, deciding upon whether to order one or two croissants, when the man sitting two tables down from me suddenly bolted.

"Hey!" called Claude from the doorway. "Stop! You haven't paid!"

I shot after him. He was a short, rotund man, with powerful legs and they were pumping like pistons. I ran as fast as I could.

The run-off had decided that fleeing down the road, rather than the narrow footpath, was a faster getaway. We were both nearly hit by various assortments of cars, motorbikes and trucks. Horns blared. Drivers screamed abuse.

After two blocks, further along Rue Rossini, he slowed. All the walking and sparring I'd been doing these past few weeks had surprisingly kept me fit. I caught him up around a corner as he half stopped to take a breather. I grabbed him by the shirt front.

"You owe Claude money, mate!"

"You're wrong. It wasn't me," he protested. What is it with these people? Standing with a knife in their hand, over three blood spattered corpses, they'd still deny it.

I was in no mood for niceties. I wrapped my right arm around him and put him in a headlock. I wedged him between myself and the side of the building. With my left hand, I found my mobile and managed to find the contact for L'Opera Mozart.

"Claude! How much did he owe you?"

Claude answered, though I didn't hear him, for this other idiot was now standing next me and he shouted, "Hey! Leave him alone!"

"Mind your own business, mate!" I snapped back. He came for me and grabbed at my right arm. With my hip, I wedged the run-off tighter against the wall. He moaned loudly. I pushed the interfering clown away, who then sprang back and tossed a punch at me. I pulled my head quickly out of the way. He slipped on the footpath and with his momentum he smacked his fist into the wall. He screamed and stumbled off wringing his right hand.

I dialled Claude again, shouting into my mobile, "How much?"

"You dropped out. A poor connection?" asked Claude.

"How much!" I reiterated. I was in no mood for explanations.

"Nine-fifty."

I hung up. I said to my still struggling captive. "Nine-fifty—get it out."

He somehow found a ten euro note. I took it, let go of him and walked off.

"Hey! Where's my change?" He called after me.

"Don't you remember? You left the café owner a tip!"

*

It was Friday evening and I'd had a shave and found a freshly ironed shirt. It was a classy dark grey and I looked okay in it. I winked at my suntanned face in the mirror. Sexual expectation is a wonderful feeling.

On the ground floor, the elevator jolted to a halt.

"Off on a hot date?" From behind his desk, M'sieur Pom watched me exit the elevator and walk towards him. He mockingly wolf-whistled. "Last week you didn't come home. I thought about calling the police. You disappeared for three days."

"Are you my mother?" I asked, mocking his concern for me.

"Someone needs to keep an eye out for you."

"Why's that?"

"A detective was asking after you."

I stopped. "Really? Did he say 'why'?"

"No. He knocked on the door of Madame Legrande."

"Is she back from hospital?" M'sieur Pom nodded that she was. "What's she done to warrant a visit from the police? Does she head a syndicate for stolen wheelchairs?"

"He's her son. He often drops in," M'sieur Pom explained.

Then it made sense. He'd been the gentleman sitting outside her hospital room.

"If anyone calls, I'll be home tomorrow after seven in the morning." I winked and started to leave. I turned back. "Yes, I am on a hot date."

"Ooh-la-la," he said, admiringly. He indicated with his head, back to the apartment behind his desk, back to his unseen wife. "I, too, once used to stay out all night. If she's worth keeping, you're going to need a steady job."

"Now, you sound like my father." I wished him well and headed off to escort Francine home. She'd be waiting for me in a bar in the Old Town, which I needed to find on my phone app. I hoped she was as keen as I was.

*

"I'm under no illusions. You'll tire of me one day." Francine was standing at her window, looking out. She had on a short silk Chinese jacket, which highlighted her legs and ageless figure. The unlit living room failed to hide the appeal of her silhouetted features.

"I don't think so," I said, sipping red wine.

She turned from the view. "I know so. Some younger woman will come along." It was like she was paving the way for me to leave her. I had no intention to—nor to even consider it.

Was she having second thoughts? The only second thought I had was to carry her to her bed once again.

I held the wine glass to my lips, not drinking, and looked at her silhouette, swaying alluringly before me. I confessed, "Younger women—they're self-centred. They require too much attention."

"I might be the older type that requires too much attention." She walked to me, took the glass from my hand and straddled me.

"Yes, you already are, but only at the times you dictate."

I squeezed her buttocks, then rubbed my hands up inside her lingerie, caressing her back. I slid them back down and firmly held her buttocks once more. I pressed her into my groin.

I asked innocently, "Why would a beautiful woman want to brand herself with a tattoo of a *fleur-de-lis* on her ass?" I playfully slapped hers.

I don't think it was the gentle slap, but something made Francine stiffen.

Chapter 9

I spent Saturday pottering. I washed down the kitchen walls and cleaned the oven. I planned what I'd like to do with the bathroom—making some sketches. I was intending only cosmetic changes, not structural. There are far too many hassles involved when relocating water pipes.

In the afternoon, I wandered over to Remy's warehouse and we danced around each other, throwing well-timed punches, most of which only connected with air.

That evening I set out looking for the Vlatava-Elbe. My research, courtesy of the one web entry on my mobile's internet listing, described it as a café, a bar and a restaurant. I guess once there, there was no need to go anywhere else. I'd found its location on my phone map, however I didn't want to walk directly to it, as I wanted to give myself, and anyone else observing me, the sense I'd accidentally stumbled upon it.

On the way there, I was wondering. If I found the Czech driver there, would I walk straight up and thump the living daylights out of him? Or do it on a darkened street, following him home? Or wait to see what he had to say for himself? A good beating was all I could give him for dumping Eloise and I needed to do something to ease the haunting look of those green eyes which often came to me at night.

The chauffeur was sitting at a table on the footpath. On his table were two plates waiting to be cleared. Perhaps his companion was inside. I decided to take my third option—I'd wait—for after careful consideration, I reasoned that I didn't need to be set upon by the entire Czech population of Nice, who were probably drinking inside.

I walked by him and stopped. I turned and put my fingers to my lips trying to recall where I'd seen his face before. I pointed at him wondering where. He caught my quizzical look.

"Cannes. I am the driver," he explained. "I gave you a card."

"Yes!" I clicked my finger in recognition. "Sorry, didn't recognise you out of uniform." I deliberately looked up at the awning of the café. I took in the signage. "Ah"—I pointed—"that makes sense."

"Care to join me for slivovitz?" He raised his small glass of clear potent liquor, and gulped it back.

I said, "No—I really should keep moving." I shook his hand. "Nice seeing you again." I started to walk off and stopped several paces away. I turned. "Oh—what the hell—yes—sounds good. I've heard of it, but never tasted it."

"Czech slivovitz is the best in the world. It's a medicine. It cures everything—including universal 'wife's nagging disease'." He laughed.

"What was that?" said a woman sitting herself down beside him at the table.

"Nothing. Nothing, my sweet. This is my wife, Ulna. I'm Milovic."

"Dougay," I said sitting. "Pleased to meet you."

Milovic turned to the open doorway, behind him. "Milos! Milos! *Dva slivovitz!*"

I was being honest when I said I'd only heard of the stuff and hadn't drunk it. We clinked glasses, toasted each other with a 'salut!' and knocked it back in one thrust. It had a kick, though it didn't taste too bad. Being well-mannered, I tried not to gasp. Milovic laughed and shouted again. "Milos! *Dva beers*—and more slivovitz!"

Ulna said something in Czech and stood. Milovic asked a question. She replied with something that made him laugh. She smiled, nodded 'farewell' to me and left.

I looked puzzled at the exchange. He said, "My wife said I have to find my own way home. I asked her: why should I come home? She said, because you have to put out the garbage next Wednesday." He laughed again.

We drank our beers and this time I *sipped* the slivovitz. I sat appreciating the aftertaste of the liqueur, slowly turning the shot glass between my fingers. He tapped his empty glass on the table.

"I'll get these," I said and stood. Before I could move off to the bar inside, Milos placed two more in front of us. I was becoming overwhelmed by Czech 'generosity'!

I was no longer planning on hitting him; however, I was still planning on asking the Czech chauffeur some questions. I hoped I'd be able to remember the answers—though I was going to have to remember the questions first.

We sat there getting happily plastered in the warm evening air. A woman walked by and Milovic said something in Czech, leaning into me.

"Does that mean—'what a honey'?" I asked, hoping for a correct translation.

He burst out laughing. "Yes, my friend! That it does! That it does! Like Belinda Swann," he said, and lifted his glass to her.

"Who's Belinda Swann?" I asked, faking ignorance.

He looked at me unbelievingly. "The actress! You know, the one who blasts those monsters from outer space?" He made a firing motion with his hands and added the sound effects with his voice. I nodded, appearing only to half follow. "What a job I have. Ten days so far. I am on call—though not tonight—I am their exclusive driver."

"Their?" I asked.

"Her husband's in Nice as well—Calvin deMarko."

I nodded. "I've heard of him."

"I took them all over. Cannes, Monaco, sightseeing along the Corniche and up the mountain to Eze."

"You don't get tired of waiting by the car while they have a good time? That was my problem back in Sydney. I wanted to go through the museums with the guests." I was now too drunk to admonish myself for lying.

"Patience, my friend. This job requires great driving skill and patience. Do it right and sometimes you get a healthy cash surprise."

I sipped the remnants of my beer.

He called behind himself. "Milos! *Dva slivovitz!*" At this rate I might have to stay the night. Though, I could probably stumble home, if I knew in which direction to walk.

"I did something I shouldn't have done," confided Milovic. "Ssshh!" Milos placed the two clear shot glasses in front of us as well as two beers which I don't remember either of us ordering.

Milovic leant forward. "I let Cal—that's Calvin deMarko—drive." I looked surprised. "Yes. Don't tell a soul. I could lose my job."

"He drove okay? Didn't damage the car?"

"No, no damage. I was with him. It was at night, no one could tell it was him behind the wheel after I put my cap on his head. We all laughed about that. I got to sit in the rear seat with the beautiful Belinda Swann!"

"Why not sit upfront, in case something went wrong? Apart from wanting to be in the back seat with…"

"His old school friend sat there. Calvin drove the Corniche. They wanted to see where Grace Kelly had died. Hollywood types—you know, under the cover of darkness, away from the eyes of the paparazzi. They got out and stood there. I sat in the car watching the three of them. She stood between them, arms around them both, holding the two men to her."

Or keeping them separated, I thought.

"They just stood there looking out over the black Mediterranean, taking it all in, like they were in a kind of prayer. I do not know. Maybe she wanted to pick up some of the Princess's acting tips. Who knows with Americans—they are so religiously obsessed—and the wackier, the better, it seems to me."

"That's no big deal—letting him drive, I said, trying to soothe his concern. "You were there keeping an eye on the car. I hope the reward was worth it."

He smiled, knowingly, as if we were fellow conspirators. "Yes, well rewarded. A couple of nights later—real money came my way." He looked about and gestured that I lean in. I did. "It was their wedding anniversary and they wanted to go somewhere and you, you know—"

"What about their hotel room?"

"Well, they didn't exactly explain to me. Their friend, the other man, did. Name?" He clicked his fingers, trying to recall. "Beau! He asked me, if he could drive the car. It was to be a special treat for Belinda. I was not to tell them, not to say anything about him having the car. It was their wedding anniversary and they'd first done it in the back of Calvin's old car, back home before they both became stars."

"And they wanted to recreate the moment?" I offered.

"Exactly," he said. "So, I gave him the car. It must have been some night. The travel rug I keep under the front seat has disappeared and there was, you know—stuff on the back seat."

"Stuff?"

"Yeh—bodily fluids."

"They screwed in the back seat of the hire car, while their friend drove it around the streets of Nice?"

"Haven't you ever wanted to?" asked Milovic, surprised. I knocked back the slivovitz and sipped the beer. Milovic went on. "I doubt it was really for them. The next day when I picked them up at their hotel and drove them to that film producer's yacht, they didn't say a thing. No thank you; no wink; nothing—like it didn't happen. Which makes me think, maybe it didn't. You see their friend is gay— outwardly gay. Maybe he went down to the old harbour— and picked up a 'hitchhiker'. You know what I mean?"

"How long did this friend of theirs have the car for?"

"It was late at night—two hours and then some. I came here. He dropped the car back to me well after midnight. He made a point of telling me that they had a great time. As he walked off, I told him to wish them happy anniversary. With a woman like Belinda Swann, who wouldn't have a great time?"

He became sentimental, the slivovitz at last having some effect. "When I was young, did young women look anything like they do today?" he mused. I waited for him to go on. He drifted out of his brief reverie. "It was worth it—one thousand euro."

"What, he wrote you a cheque?" I asked, acting dumb.

"No. He tossed me a wad in a clip. Americans! Everyone else in the world uses a wallet, but they have to use a money clip. I didn't care. Why do you think my wife's being so friendly towards me? I bought her a new dress." He laughed, and lifted his glass, cheerfully saying, "And you—I bought you some slivovitz!"

I was thankful I didn't have a wife, because in the state I was in, if I came home like this, I'd be divorced by midday tomorrow.

"Mind you, I hardly slept that night," he said.

"Worrying what you'd done—lending the car? Because you hadn't kept an eye on it?"

"No. It took a long time to clean the upholstery. Those gays sure know how to party."

Chapter 10

I found myself by the sea. Maybe it was my Australian upbringing, for somehow, I seemed to have sniffed my way automatically towards it. I recalled once seeing an old man with some bent wire in his hands divining for water. The wire had suddenly turned forwards and downwards and his mate had dug where it pointed. After a while, there was mud on the end of the spade. I remembered people applauding and tossing coins into a hat. It must have been at a sideshow or something like that.

I'd managed to find the water in a similar way, only no one tossed me coins. A policeman on patrol kicked my leg awake as I'd fallen asleep on a bench. "I'm not drunk," I said automatically, as I stumbled off. Who was I kidding?

I went down onto the rocky beach and stripped to my underpants. I fell in the water, sobering instantaneously and shouting to relieve the sudden impact of cold. I dried myself on my shirt and found my way to Place Mozart. On the way I fantasised about setting up a guided walking tour of Nice for tourists. I sure knew the best routes.

It was late Saturday or early Sunday at the height of the tourist season on the French Riviera, and I was so focused on getting home without collapsing in the gutter, I didn't remember passing anyone in the street! My new old bed never felt better.

I woke around ten and hoped Claude had a remaining croissant. He did. I washed it down with two cups of coffee. "You look terrible," he sympathised. "Out with anyone worthwhile?"

I had to pause a moment to recall where I was last night. "Now I remember—an old Czech friend."

"Good beer, Czech beer," Claude conceded. For a Frenchman, that was magnanimous praise.

"I don't remember the taste of it. I think the slivovitz washed it away."

"Oohh—now there's a drink to avoid," he advised. I nodded, agreeing. "Feel like washing up tonight? Lover boy's going to church."

"Sure, I'll be here—about five?"

In the afternoon, I managed to take the crowded train to Villefranche-sur-Mer. Sadly, Francine was nowhere to be seen. There were plenty of other beautiful women to appreciate. So I did. I swam some laps; floated on my back; allowed the sun to work its magic. I headed back to Nice and L'Opera Mozart.

After washing up and sweeping out the café, I headed around the corner for home. I found a rag and wiped down the remaining sections of living room wall I hadn't completed this past week. I looked at my aging bathroom and promised it that one day I'd get around to sprucing it up. I didn't console my kitchen. It knew it had to wait, as my meagre funds were not going to stretch that far. I had an early night.

*

"Hello?" I muttered into my mobile, half-asleep.

"Have you seen this morning's paper?" It was Jules St Croix, the disorganised private investigator.

"No."

"Get a copy. Our photograph's on the front page."

I found a copy and ordered a coffee at L'Opera Mozart. I was surprised to see Marcel serving.

"How was church?" I asked.

He replied, "You put my knives and forks away in the wrong places. I like knives on the left and forks on the right." I waited for him to laugh; however he was serious. I realised I'd just been told to improve my kitchen skills whenever I subbed for him. Francine had a much better line in reprimand.

"I'll have black coffee, thanks, lover boy."

Marcel bristled. "Only Claude calls me that."

"Sorry, but that's what everyone calls you along Le Petit Marais Nicois." That was the gay area of Nice.

Marcel went off in a huff—maybe they did call him that, as he didn't deny it.

I picked up the paper. The headline read: *Deputy Mayor Votes Away from Home.*

There was one of the photographs Jules had taken, spread across the front page as he had said. It wasn't the one where you saw the girl's tattooed ass. It was the one where she was captured face down, doing exactly what she'd been paid to do. Only her bare back and blonde hair was visible and of course the look of surprised shock on the gentleman's face as we'd burst in. There was no sign of the dog that was about to leap on me and try to eat me for breakfast.

I looked over the article. I had to guess a lot of what it said, so I asked a stranger next to me to summarise what it contained. It seems the political plans and machinations of the highly regarded Deputy Mayor, Pierre Deschamps, were now in disarray.

Marcel put down my coffee. "It was two, wasn't it?"

"No. No sugar for me."

"I meant drops of spittle."

I looked at him. "You bitch!" I said in my best offended gay voice. He sniggered and muttered something derogatory, and returned inside. I had a feeling we were never going to be friends.

I looked at the photo again. Underneath it read, *Continued on page 6*. I turned there and once again couldn't read any of it. I carried it to Claude, who dropped his tea towel and read to me.

Deputy Mayor Deschamps, with a brilliant career in front of him, was a well-respected family man. He had two grown children; his society wife, Felicity, said 'they were both trying to work their way through these trying times, but hoped that their marriage could prove to be resilient'—blah, blah, blah. The only excuse not offered was that the politician's waywardness had been caused by health problems.

Clearly there were no health issues here, for if there were, he'd be dead from a heart attack, after what that blonde had done to him. I thanked Claude for his assistance.

It is strange seeing a newspaper article and realising you knew the person in it. I didn't know him, but I knew the blonde, and I recalled her criticism of my cooking.

I ate my croissant and turned back to get another look at her. I lingered, appreciating her beauty, and seeing in my mind her sitting on the couch in that writer's apartment. I turned over the page and froze. A mug-shot of her stared back at me. It had been taken a few years earlier, however I was certain it was her. The caption read: *Dead Woman Found*. I was able to read that! I took it back inside to Claude.

The blonde was Danielle Hubert, a social worker. She'd been found under a pile of rubbish on a garbage dump.

"A garbage dump! What a place to end up in—discarded along with society's waste," said Claude, sympathetically.

I returned to my table outside, sitting back and revisiting my time with her. I saw her sitting with her legs tucked up underneath herself, flicking through her mobile; and sadly, I thought of the years she'd been denied.

I studied the photograph, still not quite believing. I saw her leaving the apartment and breezily heading to the sea. I leant in to my neighbour, and apologised once again.

He read, "Anyone with details or information about the young woman is requested to call the police." I didn't.

I wandered over to Place Mozart and wondered if I was the only person who knew the link between the two articles. Maybe there was one other—the person who'd sent her on the job to satisfy the needs of the Deputy Mayor—that person would know the unidentified woman in the bed on page one, was the same woman found in the garbage on page two. The cops wouldn't know.

Why do you kill a first-class prostitute? It's never about the actual service, because from what I've been told, the standard of service is in the title. No, I guess you kill her for what she knows or what she sees or what she puts together about clients and their friends and acquaintances and their perversions. Or you kill her because of *your* perversion. I thought again of Eloise and the scratches down the sides of her body.

I checked the article, trying to decipher it. I was sure there was no mention of scratches or *fleur-de-lis* tattoos or anything specific. The brief article only stated that she was a blonde woman in her mid-twenties, her name and occupation. No family connections were made. However, both girls, who now occupied my thoughts, were still someone's daughter.

"Perversions," I said aloud. I tapped my knee. I felt sure someone had needed to cover up a perversion. Or the perversion was carried too far. That's why Danielle was dead.

I recalled the marks around Eloise's wrists and ankles and the choke bruises on her neck. I hoped Eloise was safe or had left town.

Chapter 11

"Did you buy this morning's paper, M'sieur Pom?" I'd come inside from Place Mozart and noticed the caretaker sitting where he always was—behind the front desk, perched on his raised chair.

"Always," he explained. "I have it delivered."

"Have you kept the front page?" I asked, hoping he had.

"Why do you ask?" He pointed. "What's that under your arm?"

"There's two photographs I'd like to cut out and keep, but they're printed on either side of each other."

He nodded, and went into his apartment. He returned. "You know these two women?" He had no reason to have made the connection.

"No, but on some lonely rainy night, I'd like to," I offered as a lame excuse.

He laughed and winked. "Wait here." He returned inside. He came back with a magazine which he placed quickly in my hand. "For rainy nights—and sunny mornings!" He clicked his tongue and winked again.

"Thanks." I really didn't want the magazine—I had Francine. I tried to walk off. His voice kept me there.

"It's very interesting—this business with the Deputy Mayor. Here is a man, well-connected, well-liked—for a politician—whose age seems to be perfectly timed."

M'sieur Pom sensed that I didn't understand.

"He has time to prove himself; time to climb the ladder; maybe one day even running for President. Why does a political up-and-comer go and get himself photographed with a blonde going down on him? A little too careless of him, I say."

Before I could reply, he added, "Someone, somewhere has it in for him—or wants to stifle his ambitions. How did the photographer possibly get in?"

I remembered the door being unlocked.

"If I was in there with a blonde on top of me, I'd make sure the door was locked; every window was locked; the curtains were drawn; the phone was off the hook; I'd left my mobile at home…"

"You're an overly cautious man, M'sieur Pom."

"That I am, that I am. Then again, I've never had a blonde such as her to distract my thoughts."

I nodded. I knew what he was saying. "You're far too clever for the job you do," I said, complementing him.

"Not clever—just been around many years and seen and heard many things."

"And have you *really* heard and seen things, M'sieur Pom?"

He tapped the side of his head. "Not necessarily before my own ears and eyes, however I do love to read. Don't misunderstand me—I'm no gossip. For some reason, these nefariously suspicious activities—over the years—have stuck with me." He again tapped, with more deliberation, the side of his head. "I can remember names and faces, though sadly being a mere caretaker, stuck behind this desk in an unexciting part of Nice, I'm unable to correctly know the stories which connect them all."

I waited for him to go on.

"Supposition—in here. I have much supposition." He tapped his head a third time. "I guess it allows me to fantasise—and it keeps me off the streets!" He laughed ironically at his bout of self-awareness.

Upstairs in my room, I tossed the magazine onto the sofa and found a pair of scissors in the kitchen. M'sieur Pom's copy of the front page had not been creased like mine, so I cut around it and pinned it onto my noticeboard. The 'buy milk' note was still there. I found a pen and added: 'Bread, Cheese and German sausage.'

I cut around my copy of Danielle's mug-shot on page two and tacked it to the noticeboard as well. It wasn't a shrine I was making, just a sort of visual memory. I had no intention of putting a lit candle there and kneeling in front of it in adoration. I just felt I wanted to remember her for a while. After all, I may well be the only one who was missing her.

I sat on the sofa and picked up the magazine—*Girls of the Riviera*. I didn't know they printed this stuff anymore. I thought it would have all gone online by now. I looked at the date—it was published six years ago. On the bottom of the page it read: *Farewell Edition*.

*

In the afternoon, I went for a swim and regularly checked my mobile. There was no message from Francine; or Claude; or Jules—no offer of employment.

All the times I'd walked to the water, I rarely recognised people—each day there seemed to be a new collection out on the footpaths. I recognised the café owners on the corners where I'd pass, however I never saw anyone I knew or anyone I'd seen, say, the previous week. Of course I'd often see the same family, the collection of noisy and ill-behaved children demanding of their parents and grandparents, and only then for a few days. Once their short holiday was over, they disappeared forever. I suppose I was wondering where the locals were.

However, this morning I saw a man I'd seen before, though when, I couldn't recall. He walked with a purpose; he was in no hurry; his eyes rarely seemed to deviate from straight ahead. He was tall and thin and wore unfashionable clothes. I couldn't criticise him on that account, as I was hardly dressed by Yves Saint-Laurent. He was just one of those people you noted and remembered. Amongst the crowd, effortlessly gliding forward, cutting through them, I noticed he did not stop and start, nor stumble, because of their presence in his path. For future reference, I dubbed him 'The Walking Man'.

I try not to drink alcohol on a Monday evening—I'd decided a long time ago, after a very heavy long weekend in Sydney, that I needed at least one night a week off the drink to preserve my liver, so I cooked a stir fry and then as the sun faded, I took myself off for a walk. I'd done a lot of that since arriving in Nice. I was happy with that, because that's how a stranger learns the layout of his new hometown—

appreciating buildings, then as they became familiar, ignoring them. Now I was sober, I'd given up on the idea of setting up a walking tourist business.

Down by the old port area, a car stopped behind me and the passenger alighted. It drove by me. It was an old Renault—the type with the gearstick in the dashboard. I'd never seen one in the flesh. There weren't any of those back in Australia that I could recall ever coming across. It appeared to have been lovingly restored. I was impressed. The driver got out and looked up at the street numbers.

I was grabbed from behind and held. As I struggled with my assailant, the driver in front ran to me and hit me in the stomach several times with all his force. The man behind ferociously pulled back my arms putting his knee in my back. The driver thumped me another three, four times, higher up on my chest area, building on the impacts he'd made. I was positioned like the heavy bag in a boxing gym—like that one I found at Remy's—and they were taking full advantage of it.

The one behind let go of one arm and as I half-spun, he smacked my ear with all his force. My brains seemed to spin. From behind, my neck and shoulder were given a savage chop and finally the one in front laid his knee into my groin and I let out a deep heartfelt "Ooaarrr!" They let me fall to the road. They quickly walked off to the Renault. I tried to catch a glimpse of the number plate. I couldn't focus my eyes. Down there, in the prayer position, I asked God whether I was still capable of producing children.

That pain is a pain like no other. I stayed there, wishing it would ease, catching my breath before I tried to find my feet. They were still at the end of my legs. It was no time for humour, however that seemed to be the only thing I could think of to try to relieve the pain. I'd never been worked over. I knew how to throw a punch—in a contest between two equally paired fighters—but this was different—it was all over before I even clenched my fist.

It was a Monday night—the night I didn't drink—so I stumbled to Vlatava-Elbe. I didn't expect to find Milovic, I just wanted to test his theory that slivovitz could be used for medicinal purposes. After Milos brought the third one, I believed it could.

Back home, I added "Toothpicks" to my shopping list and stripped slowly, uttering several groans. I stood in front of the mirror. I was heavily bruised—that was no surprise—it was the amount of bruising I had, turning my skin black, which surprised me. Maybe they'd hit me more times than I remembered. I stood and pissed away the slivovitz; got changed into my unflattering kangaroo pictured T-shirt to sleep in; and crashed. I heard my mother ask me if I'd remembered to clean my teeth. I lied—I told her I had. I pulled up the pink duvet and groaned ironically to myself, "*Bon nuit*, mate!"

Chapter 12

I stayed in bed Tuesday morning. With every move I made, something, somewhere inside me ached. When I tried to roll over, it ached more and I groaned to match the motion. After a few minutes of this, I managed to sit upright—stage one completed—and then I pushed up through my legs and walked to the bathroom—stage two completed. Stage three saw me relieve myself and return to the protection of my alluring duvet. "Thank you, Princess Grace," I moaned out loud, falling back asleep.

Around eleven, I took the shopping list and gingerly headed out, via L'Opera Mozart for an anticipated 'I'm-still-alive-coffee'; then to the small neighbourhood supermarket. I bought what I'd written on my list and managed to find sandpaper, hidden on a shelf down the rear of the store.

Once back home, I ate a slice of melted cheese on toast and began to sandpaper the walls in the living room. Over the coming weekend, I thought I might paint them a deep cream. The skirting boards would have to wait until I had a little more money set aside, for I wanted to do them in white enamel. The sandpapering took all the afternoon—raising an arm was not achieved without pain.

That night I cooked the German sausage and covered it in fried tomatoes and onions, liberally coated with soya sauce. I hadn't come across an Asian restaurant yet, and being Australian, I was starting to crave the flavours of the mystic orient. I slept long and deep.

The next morning, after a late coffee and croissant at L'Opera Mozart, I returned home to wipe down the walls from yesterday's sandpapering. I was feeling a little less achy, so a wipe down, a swim and an afternoon nap were on my agenda for the day—unless Francine rang with a job offer.

There was a knock at the door. It was M'sieur Pom. "Madame Legrande wonders if you could come down, please."

"She's okay? Nothing wrong?"

"Everything is fine. She'd just like to see you." I washed and wiped my hands and followed the old caretaker to the elevator.

*

M'sieur Pom knocked on the apartment door of Madame Legrande. The door opened. Her well-dressed son stood there and smiled at us.

"Thank you, M'sieur Pom—my regards to your wife." He gave the old man ten euro.

"Thank you, Monsieur." The caretaker returned to his desk, pocketing his windfall.

"Come in, Monsieur Roberre." He extended his hand and I shook it. He lightly placed his hand upon my back as I walked through the small, floor tiled entranceway. I immediately had the feeling that he was in control. No matter what the situation, I felt he would always be in control.

The apartment was unlike mine. It was spacious and plush—exquisitely decorated and furnished. I could have lived for several years off the cost of the chandelier alone.

Two women were seated on a finely crafted sofa. One I knew, of course—Madame Legrande—the other was a stranger.

"Ah—Dougay—come in, come in." My conversational partner from Place Mozart was bright and sparky this morning.

"Are you well, Madame? Your stay in hospital is well and truly behind you?"

She said that it was, rising to kiss me on both cheeks.

"Let me introduce you," began her well-dressed son. "This is Madame Ardoin. And I must, of course, introduce myself, though no doubt Maman has spoken of me—I am Pierre."

"Hello, Pierre. No—I hate to disappoint you," I said, trying to lighten the tension I could feel in the room. "Your mother rarely speaks of you two boys, other than to say she adores you, and you in return adore her."

As if to reinforce my observation, Madame Legrande hugged her son as she turned back to me and asked, "Tea? Yes?" She then explained to us all, "I'm afraid many years ago, I fell for the English habit of drinking tea. Mind you, it is the only thing of theirs I fell for." She was in her element. Guests were in her apartment; she was playing the hostess; and she was demonstrating she'd lost none of her conversational humour. She went to the kitchen, Pierre saying to me, "Sit, please sit."

I did so and smiled at the woman opposite.

"Madame Ardoin has asked a favour of me and I would like to pass on that favour to you," explained Pierre, as reason for having me brought down.

"I wish to pay you for it," explained the woman.

Pierre went on, slightly irritated that he'd been interrupted. "You would not let me offer you anything at the hospital for saving my mother's life."

"Oh, the doctors saved your mother's life, Monsieur, not me."

"Nevertheless your quick actions meant that she is as she is today. I wish to reward you, and so I felt that a job for me—well, for Madame Ardoin here—might satisfy both of our sensibilities."

I knew to limit my resistance when money was dangled before me.

"Perhaps, I can have Madame explain," said Pierre.

The woman shifted a little on the sofa, preparing to begin. She cleared her throat. "Monsieur Roberre, my niece has gone missing. My sister has not heard from her in nearly two weeks."

Pierre spoke, "Dougay, I have people in my employ who could possibly find a trace of her—however—well, according to M'sieur Pom, you may be able to use the money."

"You see, Monsieur, she did hang about with a dubious crowd," clarified Madame Ardoin. "Though she is my niece—we love her dearly…"

"And if she's fallen foul of this crowd," continued Pierre, "neither of us wants to be tarnished in any way." He eased into me. "Dougay, you are new here in Nice and over times past, my name has been wrongly and unfairly linked to some—well, not too pleasant activities."

"For me it's a delicate family matter," admitted Madame Adroin. "You see, we are well known on the Cote d'Azur."

I nodded as if I understood.

Pierre spoke. "I feel—we feel—you're the perfect choice for someone to go about and make enquiries. Not wishing to offend you, Dougay, but you're no one. I mean that in the best possible sense. I asked my brother—he's a detective—and he got back to me and said no one's ever heard of you in Nice. It's as if you didn't exist here until a few weeks back."

I went to explain how that could be, however, he cut me off.

"No, no need, I'm sure you're no criminal or international fugitive." He laughed hollowly. "I feel sure you'll be able to find things, go places, my easily recognised employees won't."

I considered this. He came and stood over me, his back to Madame Ardoin. I didn't feel threatened, however, I did become wary.

He whispered, "Five hundred. A thousand if you find her." I was now less wary. He moved back and sat on the sofa with Madame Ardoin.

"If you believe I can, then I'll try," I said, smiling at both of them.

"Good." Pierre clapped his hand and patted the lady's knee in reassurance. She smiled at him, brightening up.

"What's the girl's name? I asked.

"Eloise," she said. "Eloise…" The woman hesitated.

"Pittard," added Pierre.

I sat very still. I hoped I'd not given away any perception of recognition, as a shiver ran through me. Was this a coincidence or did someone know something about me and Eloise? After she left me, was she now still missing? Had something else happened to her?

I wondered, *just how much do I need to protect myself?* Self-survival is an unappreciated trait, except for those of us who are about to tread into, or have poured over us, hot water.

"Does your mother have a pencil and paper?" I asked Pierre. "So I can take down some details? I don't have anything on me."

"I'd rather you didn't," said the woman, slightly nervously.

"I think what Madame is implying," began Pierre, "is that this search is of a very sensitive nature—it could rebound politically. The less notes on paper—the safest for us all if there are—repercussions—of a scandalous nature."

"So—ah—Eloise, you say?" I asked making out I'd nearly forgotten.

"Yes," said the concerned aunt.

"You haven't reported her missing to the police?" I asked her, then immediately to Pierre, "To your brother?"

"No." Pierre replied for the both of them. "We feel it might be safer for the girl if they weren't involved. Madame fears she may know someone or something."

He stopped and rose again. He stood over me and whispered, "Madame fears she may have been working as a call girl."

"Here's the tea!" said Madame Legrande entering. "Pierre, on the kitchen bench there are some cakes."

"Yes, *Maman*, of course." It was as if the man was twelve again.

When Pierre had left, I whispered to Madame Ardoin, "Does your niece have any identifying marks?"

"Oh—only the usual." She didn't know her niece as well as I did.

Pierre returned and we all sipped our tea and ate our cakes as if we hadn't a care in the world. It was as if every day of the week, around midday, two men and two women gathered in this apartment and smiled and exchanged pleasantries.

After a while, Pierre ushered me to the doorway. I turned to him. "How will I contact you, Pierre?"

"Dougay, ask my mother to give me a call."

"Will do."

Chapter 13

I went swimming, dried myself and returned home. I sat for about forty minutes in Place Mozart, thinking, worrying. I was no detective, so I couldn't fall back on experience. I didn't know where to start to try to find Eloise. However, I knew someone who could provide advice. Not wishing to call, I set off on foot.

"You've accepted a job doing what? You want to do me out of my career?" Jules was concerned that the apprentice was taking over.

"No. I came for advice, however, if you want to assist…"

"I'm not saying that." He calmed. "Explain."

"I've agreed to track down a missing girl."

"Report it to the police—mind you, they won't find her."

"So why should I report her?" I asked pointedly.

"True," he conceded.

"Besides, Jules, I can't—it's a delicate matter. The family is politically connected, they don't want the publicity."

"She's run off with her boyfriend," he said dismissively.

"They need to save face."

"There's nothing shameful in having a runaway in the family. It happens all the time."

"If you can't help me, then point me in the right direction." I wasn't prepared yet to mention the money I'd been offered.

He moved his head from side to side, weighing up whether to assist or not. "What's her name?" he asked.

"You won't know her."

"Try me."

"Eloise Pittard."

"You're right—for once—I don't." He sniggered at his own lame gag. "What do you know about her?"

"She's a prostitute."

"Oh great! Who cares?" He stood up and walked around the desk. He shut the door in case anyone could be possibly listening, not that there was anyone sitting in the cupboard he called his outer office. "A prostitute! Why waste your time? Look at that blonde they found on the garbage dump!"

"She's a prostitute?" I played dumb. He had not made the connection between the dumped blonde and the one in his photographs.

"Of course! Who throws away a princess?" He waited for my answer. There was none. He went on, thinking I hadn't understood his illusion. "No one tosses away anything of value. Only lowly prostitutes get discarded in such a fashion. Why do they want you to find a working girl?"

"What I said is true. She's the daughter and a niece of two concerned women. Come on, Jules, even a call girl has a family."

"Okay, okay, Monsieur Righteousness." He gave in and returned to his commanding position behind his desk. "What else?"

"She's beautiful; dark hair; green eyes; mid-twenties."

"Of course, she is," he said cynically. "She's the whole one hundred and ten percent fantasy. Okay—pass over the photograph—let me see her."

"I don't have a photograph."

"What?" His head suddenly straightened. "You're looking for a missing woman and you don't have a photograph? Didn't you ask for one?"

"No."

"Didn't they give you one?"

"No."

"How stupid are you?" He waited for a reply—I wasn't going to give him one. "No wonder you need my help. Wait! How do you know what she looks like?"

"I've met her."

"You've fucked her? How much?"

"No, I haven't and what difference does the price make?"

"It lets me know if she's high-class or low-class. Looking at you I'd say low-class—very low-class." He laughed again at his own joke.

"I saved her life."

"What? This is becoming fanciful. Get out of here— you're pulling my dick!"

"No. It's true. She has a small *fleur-de-lis* tattooed on her right buttock." Jules went suddenly quiet. "Just like that blonde—the time I wrestled that dog!"

We stared at each other. I waited for him to continue poking fun at me—he didn't.

He spoke softly. "Get out of here—and forget about finding her."

"Why?"

I waited. He didn't answer. He opened a desk drawer and took out two glasses and a bottle of vodka. He poured the two glasses. He passed one to me. He raised his and I raised mine and we clinked. He said, "It's been nice knowing you." He knocked back the vodka. I didn't.

"Jules—what are you saying?"

"Have you just come down in the last shower? Where've you been all your life?"

"In Australia."

"Yes. I'd forgotten," he admitted. "You need to attend a lecture on the recent social history of Nice. And I have neither the time, nor the inclination, to deliver it."

I knocked back the vodka and slumped back, defeated. He read my body language.

"Okay, okay. Women tattooed with a *fleur-de-lis* are very, very high-class. They only service the wealthy and connected. It's a small group—maybe six or eight women. I don't really know—how could I? They are heavily protected, well-groomed and cared for. Like some mythical society. Do not mess in that circle. You do not want to stumble across Pierre Legrande."

Now it was my turn to be shocked. Jules was right about me not understanding Nice's recent past. I had no idea of the nature of the tentacles woven through its tapestry. I wondered how I was going to tell him. Break it to him gently or just blurt it out? I blurted out, "That's who's asked me to find her."

"What?" He looked incredulously at me. "How'd you find him? Or rather—how'd he find you?"

"I know his mother."

"Bullshit! Fucking bullshit!" He fell silent. He drank directly from the bottle. "I can't help you, Dougay. You're on your own."

"I know a bit about the missing girl's whereabouts the moment before I saved her life."

"Forget them. In a week's time, go back to Legrande and tell him you've hit a brick wall, a dead end, tell him that the girl's disappeared off the planet."

I took his advice. However, I didn't wait a week before I went back to see Pierre Legrande.

*

Why wasn't I given a photograph of Eloise? Pierre knew I knew who she was—that's why! People gossip in every apartment block in every corner of the world. His mother would have known I'd taken a young woman in off the street. Her apartment light had come on! And M'sieur Pom knew Eloise's name, and for ten euro…

Once on the street, I called Madame Legrande. She willingly gave me her son's office address. I was going to make good use of my multi-day travel pass today, as once again I'd be criss-crossing the city. I don't like being played for a fool. It festered inside me all the way over.

Pierre's office disguised his nefarious business. It was in a building near Francine's office. On the foyer's directory, it simply read: *Legrande Enterprises, room 207.* I climbed the stairs, rather than wait for the elevator.

I opened the door and was surprised to see no receptionist behind the desk, in the outer office. Maybe she was out on a break. The desk had the usual 'receptionist/secretary' paraphernalia on it. The room was designed in the style of 'barren chic'. It was ordinary looking, too ordinary looking, for the secrets it no doubt contained in its computer files.

A large man, the man I'd seen at the hospital with Pierre, sat in a comfortable chair near the doorway of the inner office.

"Is Pierre in?" I asked.

He nodded and I crossed towards him, to the closed door of a third office. The large man stood in front of it, barring my way.

"Who is it?" I heard from inside the office.

"Dougay Roberre," I called out, bluntly.

"Enter!"

The big man opened it, letting me in by him. Pierre sat at his desk.

I wasted no time in letting fly with my invective. "What was that charade about? You know perfectly well who Eloise Pittard is! She's one of your girls! What do you take me for? You lying bastard!"

"No one speaks to me like that," said an affronted Pierre.

The large man came at me. I half stepped back and landed a perfectly timed straight left onto his jaw, turning my fist quickly to the right on impact. He fell to the floor. He didn't get up.

"My God!" uttered Pierre in disbelief. "Do you know what you've done?"

"It seems your friend here has a glass jaw." The large man did not move. "Keep your offer of money. The price for saving your mother's life is a dressing down—from me—and you've just had it! Neither of us owes the other anything. Why the world has to tolerate the presence of you shitheads is beyond me."

I turned and stormed out. I fell over the large man on the floor. Pierre laughed out loud.

As I was picking myself up, he said, "You're right. There are times when I don't have a very high opinion of myself either. Sit down. Can I get you a drink?"

I calmed. "Sure and a small glass of water for…" I indicated the lump on the carpet.

"Luigi."

I sprinkled water onto the large man's face. He came around. He looked at me surprised. Pierre stood over him. "It's okay, Luigi. Come on." To my surprise, Pierre offered him his own hand and helped him to his feet.

"Campari?" he asked. The large man nodded. "Sit—I'll get it."

Pierre poured a large drink for Luigi and beckoned that I sit on one of the comfortable leather chairs over by the window. I did.

Pierre sat and leant back, crossing his legs at the ankle. "I don't know where Eloise is. Which means she's suddenly quit my service; or scared and in hiding; or dead. I hope it's the middle reason."

"You're actually concerned about her?"

"Of course!" He was affronted by my question. "What do you take me for—a callous white slave trader?"

I let that hang.

"I haven't lied to you. I thought perhaps she'd foolishly 'fallen in love' and wanted a proper relationship. I heard you'd taken her in."

"I don't have her. Do I look like the sort of man who could keep a young woman like her happy, day and night in my attic?" He didn't answer—he didn't have to. "True—I took her in; I cleaned her up; and she stayed the night—on the sofa, not in my bed—so don't think about sending me an invoice."

"I understand all that," he said, standing. He began to pace. "I thought you might contact whoever she'd gone and shacked up with. Convince him to return her for a share of the thousand euro I offered." He drained his glass. "If you don't know, I wonder where she is then?"

I let him ponder and then asked, "What about Danielle Hubert?" I asked.

"Sadly, I know where she is."

"You don't seem overly concerned."

He stopped pacing. "Oh, I'm very concerned. However, the police are handling that—for the moment. When they give up and label it a cold case, then I may want your assistance again. I will very much want to bring that case back to life. Danielle was a special young woman. A lot of time and care and energy and money went into her—as for all of my girls. A sudden departure is very difficult to replace. A retirement I can prepare for."

I wasn't caring one fig for his business concerns.

He looked at me, as if he'd just realised something. "How did you make the connection between Eloise and Danielle?"

"The alluring brand you have your cattle stamped with."

"You've seen Danielle's naked ass?"

"Not only hers—but a redhead on a boat in Cannes. I hope she's alright."

He nodded that she was. "How did you get aboard *The Blue Dahlia*?" he asked.

"Delivering a script—doing a job for the solicitor—Francine Delange. You know her?"

"I've come across her." He thought. "Tallish, jet-black hair, good-looking woman?"

"Yes, that's the one."

"The offer still stands," Pierre said, returning to the task at hand. "I want you to find Eloise."

"Thanks for the drink," I said, standing, placing the empty glass on the coffee table before us.

"I'm very protective of all my girls." We shook hands. "You seem to shake hands a lot," he said.

"It's my Australian upbringing." I moved to the door. Luigi stood to make sure I was definitely leaving. "It's okay Luigi. No hard feelings? Your jaw—it's genetic." I offered him my hand. He glanced at his boss, who nodded. We shook hands. It was not a pleasant experience for the big Italian.

Pierre stopped me with his voice. "You see a man owns a tyre shop—for top-end cars only. Other manufacturers provide the cheap runabouts for the majority of the population. When one of those cheap providers blows one of your tyres and tries to sell their own inferior product in its place. Then there's a problem."

"Is that what you think happened to Danielle? A rival beginning to chip away at your empire?"

"I do not know. Too early to say—far too early. Find Eloise. The offer still stands—a thousand." He took a business card from his inside pocket and on the back of it scrawled a number. "That's my mobile. Very, very few people have that. Don't lose it. Put it into your phone, then tear it up—and don't lose your phone. Me, giving you that, should be an indication of my concern for the whereabouts of Eloise Pittard."

I took a step and turned. "Did you have me beaten up?"

"Beaten up?"

"Yes, set upon in the street—after dark."

"What do you take me for?" he asked. I didn't answer. "No. Why would I want to have you beaten up?"

I believed him. I moved to the door, stopping on his voice.

"How long have you been in Nice?" he asked, guiding my thinking.

"Four months," I said.

"Cross paths with anyone since then?"

I left wondering. I heard Luigi slam the door behind me.

Chapter 14

I found a bus which dropped me at Gare de Nice. Walking down to my apartment, I passed 'The Walking Man'.

"*Bonjour*," I said. He waved a half-raised arm in return, however didn't stop. I changed for the beach and spent the late afternoon swimming—and thinking.

I thought of how stupid I'd been in barging in and abusing Pierre Legrande. I recalled the fear Jules had expressed when his name was mentioned. I thought about how fortunate I'd been that Luigi had a glass jaw. Instead of swimming in water, I could well be swimming in garbage on the spot vacated by Danielle Hubert.

As the cliché goes, fools rush in—and in my case, this fool was a true innocent. Jules was right. I had no experience of the hierarchy in Nice; no idea of who to bow to; or to avoid; or be friendly with—real or false. That's what comes from having just arrived, fully formed and dropped down in the middle of other's established lives.

Then again, I thought that maybe my brashness had given me a certain respect in the eyes of Pierre Legrande.

I believed he wanted to find Eloise. I wasn't making a judgment as to the reason—though I believed that once I'd found her, he did not intend to harm her. I wanted to find

Eloise—if only to know she was okay, for I had no concern whether she'd return to her employment with Pierre; or run off with a lover who'd offered a future of safety and stability; or if she'd gone back home—to the concerned aunt and mother, who seemed to be too caught up in their social circle to fully embrace her return to the family fold.

Where would I start to find her? I had a car number plate and I had a possibility of a driver, though why such an obviously gay, overtly butch man, with a penchant for male rough stuff would want to beat up on a woman, I didn't know. Though 'beat up on' might be the reason. Maybe he hated women. Maybe Eloise had laughed at him, or derided him in public. Or she screwed a straight man he was secretly in love with? Like an old high-school buddy?

I then recalled hearing Harold Kempenski say, 'He'll do anything for his boss. A real cock sucker and arse licker'. Was Beau jealous of Calvin? But Calvin had a wife—a very public wife. Had Calvin screwed Eloise? Was that the root of Beau's jealousy and was that why she was beaten up and abused and dumped on the street? Was Calvin bisexual?

I had a thousand questions and still no place to start. One question that did mean a lot to me, for it was personal, was who had had me bashed up?

I swam long strokes and went over the very few possibilities. Claude? Why would a café owner want me bashed? I don't write restaurant reviews! Remy? I'd never complained about any of his dodgy dealings. Marcel? No, it wouldn't be Marcel. I wasn't interested in moving him aside and becoming Claude's lover!

The tourists were out in force as I walked the streets of the old town, passing by the crowded and noisy restaurants, customers spilling onto the footpaths, joyousness in the air. Tonight, I was not infected with bonhomie. I wondered if I'd ever have enough money again to go on a carefree holiday.

I sat at the familiar table at Vlatava-Elbe. Milovic wasn't there. It was Wednesday night and I hadn't expected him. He could not afford a hangover in the morning when he began driving. Milos placed a double slivovitz in front of me. I looked up at him.

He explained, "It saves me coming back a second time." He laughed.

"Any chance of a beer?" I asked. He slid it out from behind his back. He was in a good mood. He messed my hair as he returned indoors.

I knocked back half of the slivovitz and sipped some of the beer. "Lemoine!" I said out loud. "Lemoine and his ugly tart!" I drank the beer again and sat back pleased. I was sure I had the person who set those thugs on me.

Draining the shot glass and the beer bottle, I went inside and paid Milos. I stood a little unsteadily on my feet, affected by the impact of walking out into the night air again. The slivovitz had given me its usual warm glow.

I needed to be with Francine. I was in her area and soon found myself at the front door of her apartment block. I pressed her intercom.

"Hello?"

"Hi, Francine! It's me!"

There was a pause.

"It's not Friday."

"Yes, I know." I leant my arm against the wall and moved my face into the speaker, confidentially asking, "Is there any chance you want to see me?"

"No." She hung up. The intercom went dead.

I walked down to the sea and paced slowly along the promenade. Others were there, arm in arm, kissing, holding each other tightly. Children played and ran happily in front of parents, calling after them, "Hurry up!" Mobile phones flashed; happy memories were being recorded. Loneliness exists everywhere, however never is it so heartfelt as in a crowd.

The slivovitz was warm inside me and I wanted to feel her; to put my arms around her; to just be in her presence. I went back to Francine's apartment building.

"Hello?" came Francine's distorted voice through the tinny speaker.

"I think I may—love you," I confessed into the wall.

"You're drunk!" The intercom went dead again.

I walked to the station nearby and rode the train one stop. I weaved downhill to Rue Auber. Back in my apartment, I stripped and had a shower. *I've got to do something with these walls*, I thought, as the water cascaded over me. *They're starting to bubble.*

I lay in bed, with the reading lamp on. I grabbed the magazine M'sieur Pom had given me and flicked through it. Beautiful women can normally cheer me up—not tonight.

What had I said to Francine? I'd told her I thought I loved her. Did I? I certainly ached for her. That didn't matter—the point was I'd told her. And I got a very strong impression that she was not happy to hear it.

At about page seventeen, I sat up a little straighter. It wasn't the woman who'd caught my eye—though she was a stunner. It was where she was, where the photograph was taken. She was standing, hands modestly placed, with water cascading over her. She was in a shower and the shower area was covered in large cream tiles with a maroon border.

Chapter 15

Over morning coffee at L'Opera Mozart I phoned Remy. "Claude—can you turn the music down a bit? I'm trying to wheel and deal here!"

Claude called back over its volume, "You do not like *The Marriage of Figarro*, my friend?"

"No. I wasn't invited! Hello—Remy?"

"Dougay!" he sounded pleased to hear my voice. Then suspiciously, he asked, "What do you want?"

"Why would I want something?" I asked, my words dripping with false innocence.

"You only call me when you want something. Do you ever ask about me? Do you ever ask: How is the wife, Remy?"

"Your wife left you years ago."

"How do you know that? I never talk about her."

"The wonders of the internet."

"Is there nothing private anymore?" Before I could agree with him, he added, "That's why I keep the roller door down and locked! Computers can't see through steel."

"Yes, even Superman couldn't do that."

"Yes, he could. He couldn't see through *lead*!"

I accepted the correction and felt he was about to hang up. I quickly said, "I need your assistance today."

"I've got my hands full. They'll be empty about eleven-thirty."

*

I waved to Remy's CCTV camera and waited. His door didn't open. I danced a short gigue for the camera. Remy did not appear. I banged on the roller door as usual. The single steel door opened, as usual.

"Oh, it's you," he said.

"Couldn't you see me on the big screen?" I asked, pointing to the mounted camera down the end of the wall.

"That doesn't work. It's not connected."

"Then why is it…"

"The young are so gullible."

"Aren't you worried about *old* thieves?"

"I know all the old thieves in Nice and they know me. Any of them try to break in, they know I'll give them a quality thumping, professionalism guaranteed."

"Then why all the security?"

"To keep out the cops!"

Remy let me in and closed the steel door behind us. I joined him at his desk. A leather jacket lay across it, as if he'd put it there for some sort of presentation.

"Nice jacket," I commented. I felt it—it was made from very soft leather.

He looked at me, considering whether to explain the circumstances in which he happened to have it lying across his desk. "I was given it as payment. It doesn't fit me. Try it on."

"Me?" I asked incredulously.

He looked about. "Who else is in here?"

I put the black jacket on.

"Fits a treat!" he assessed. It did. I started taking it off. "No. Keep it—it's yours."

I stopped removing it. "I can't afford this."

"No, no charge. Free!"

"That's mighty generous of you." I still could not believe it. "Thank you, Remy."

"Better *you* wear the stolen goods than *me*."

I glared back at him. He laughed. "It's legit! Truly!"

I thanked him again, adding, "If there's anything I can do for you."

"You do plenty for me—you play my straight man. Now, what is it you want?"

*

Remy was unable to park his truck where he'd parked last time down at the rear of the basement because there were two other trucks parked down there. He reversed up the drive and parked on the street. We walked around. Serge had heard the old truck over-revving, climbing in reverse. He was waiting for us.

Remy nodded at him. "Serge—you remember Dougay?"

The old man did. We shook hands and formed a three-man huddle. "What's going on with the trucks?" asked Remy.

"Filming—inside." Remy nodded knowingly. Serge tapped him in the stomach. "Give me ten euro and I'll let you in to have a sneak peek. Your new bed is getting a proper workout! There's this tanned woman in there, all oiled up." He shook his hand, approvingly. "They got her with this black man—and this other pure white guy—hasn't even got a tan—what do you call them?"

"Albino," said Remy.

"That's it."

"Interesting colour combination," said Remy. I couldn't tell if he was being facetious or not. "I love racial harmony."

"I can only imagine what she's doing to the both of them." Serge shuddered a little, adding, "In the name of art, of course." Both he and Remy laughed cynically.

From my jeans pocket, I took out the picture I'd ripped from M'sieur Pom's magazine. "Is this the bathroom inside? The one in that far corner?"

Serge looked at Remy. "So you won't be paying ten euro?" he asked, disappointed.

"I'll pay you double if you answer my questions," I said. I now had Serge's attention. He looked at me, then to Remy. Remy nodded that it was okay to trust me.

"Alright, but no names," Serge said. "I don't know any—so I can't tell you—from me you'll get no names—even if I knew them." He'd made his point and I agreed to his terms and conditions. "Let's head up the street—get a coffee," he suggested.

"That might be a little too public for the answers I'm interested in." I thought Serge, like me, would want to be guarded with what he was going to say.

"Don't worry. The coffee tastes like shit. There'll be no customers there."

Serge was right.

We were huddled around a small circular metal legged table. The straight-backed chairs were also metal. There was no cushion in sight. I hoped the questions wouldn't take too long for I feared I was going to walk away with a sore ass.

"I have been the caretaker for many years. The owner of the building pays me well to look and never see." He said it simply, providing guidelines for my 'interview'.

"This photograph was taken in the basement?" I asked what I'd asked back by the building's basement. I needed to set this process in place. I didn't wish for it to devolve into two old guys reminiscing and me seeming to eavesdrop.

"Yes. I remember the session. It was the last for that magazine. It closed down—killed by the internet. You know they take so many photographs and end up using only one. That girl was a honey." He leant into us. "She did very well for herself. The magazine owner—publisher—whatever you call them—he came here for the shoot. He couldn't take his eyes off her. At the end of the shoot, he took her back to Paris. I heard he actually married her." He tapped the photograph. "Marriage—that's how I remember. Imagine waking up next to her every morning." The three of us did.

I cleared my throat, and Serge went on. "I remember one of the girls asking me: Why her and not me? I couldn't tell her 'why' because I was unable to choose between the two of them."

Clearly Serge loved his job.

"That's why I've never been a judge of bikini contests on the beach," offered Remy. "How can you choose a winner from ten bodies of perfection?"

"Remy!" I tapped the picture, yet again, trying to get the two older men's attention.

"Yes, that's the bathroom," Serge admitted without further prompting.

I sipped the foul-tasting coffee, wondering how I'd phrase my next question. I took the twenty euro out of my pocket and held it flat on the table top beneath my index finger. *Maybe this might help its formation*, I thought. I looked Serge in the eye. "Has anything ever gone wrong?"

"Wrong?" He asked, as if insulted that anything on his watch could possibly not be right.

"When Remy and I were here, I noticed blood on the Turkish carpet—washed blood on the mattress."

Serge put his index finger on the other end of the twenty euro note. "There was no blood on the carpet. That was a stain from spilt oil."

I looked at him unbelievingly.

"No, it's true. Did you sniff it?" I recalled I hadn't—I'd just assumed the worst. "They were filming these five, six women crawling over this guy—they were all oiled, he's tied to the bed and one of the women slipped off him and the bed and onto the floor. The crew laughed! Hell, I laughed! You see a crewman had placed the can of bulk oil at the foot of the bed and not far enough out of reach. She'd knocked it over when she fell. What a fuss she'd made, limping around crying—the whole works—tossing a real tantrum. I thought, what she needs is a smack on the ass!" He laughed.

"From me!" Remy laughed.

"Come on, gentlemen, concentrate!" I reprimanded.

"It wasn't blood," said Serge, focusing. "It was a simple mistake and when the shoot was over, I needed to get rid of the rug. No one was going to hire a set with that as a feature."

He tried to ease the banknote towards himself. I pushed down on it. It wasn't going anywhere yet.

"And the stain on the mattress? That was blood, wasn't it?"

Serge dropped his voice. "Well—that experience was not as funny. Two gigs on the same day—when the filming was over, that night another 'hire' came in. They couldn't have cared less about the rug being stained with oil. I don't think they even turned on a light. I was outside and I don't remember seeing anything come on through the high window. Between those two sessions, I scraped off as much oil as I could. Yes, it was blood on the mattress."

"Someone was killed there? On the bed Remy and I took away?"

"No, no, no. Not killed," said Serge, sure that was not the reason. "Menstrual blood. It was blood of a virgin."

Did I believe him? It wasn't Danielle's blood?

I persisted. "No one was killed here—like a beautiful blonde woman?"

"Is that your fantasy?" asked Serge. I made no reply. "No. The girl walked away—alive. They knocked on the roller door and I opened it. She was helped to the car." I was about to let go of my end of the twenty euro note, however Serge continued. Perhaps he needed to ease his conscience.

"He was a conceited asshole. Most rich Americans are. Big shot, you know. Fly over here, fuck our women—in his case our underage flowers—toss some bucks their way—then fly back. Hell, that asshole literally tossed the cash at me, after they'd stowed her in the back seat. They drove off and I had to bend down to pick up the crumpled money. I went back to tidy the set and I tried to wash the blood off. Impossible."

"What did they look like?"

"I can't give you any names—I don't know who they are—honestly!"

"No names," I agreed. I remembered, like Serge, bending down to pick up my crumpled money on *The Blue Dahlia*.

"The American was a solid, stocky man—a bull of a man—in his fifties. The other man, the driver, never said a word. He held back. He oversaw everything—hired muscle, too many steroids. He pranced, rather than walked. He never participated in the underage sex. I thought he was gay—you know, a man with too many muscles, too in love with himself, to be appealing to too many women."

This was not what I was expecting to hear. I came hoping to learn of the last minutes of Danielle Hubert, even have confirmation of the scene of Eloise's assault.

I let go of the twenty euro. Serge slid it into his palm.

"The girl was sobbing, trying to keep the tears in," he said, reflecting. "I remember that. I still hear her some nights."

Chapter 16

That night I walked along the street, passing Lemoine's ground floor apartment. Behind the front roomed curtain, a standard lamp had been turned on. In the twenty minutes I stood nearby, no shadows crossed it. I assumed they weren't in. To ease my boredom, I moved further across the street and down a little. I waited some more. I had assumed correctly.

Lemoine and his tart wandered along the street emerging from the shadows behind me—hardly the loving couple—for she was chewing him out about something he didn't do or never considered doing. I caught the phrase, "You always let me down."

Waiting until they'd unlocked their door, I ran over and turning my left shoulder, slammed into the back of them both, knocking them inside to the floor. I slammed the door behind us.

"I'll make it simple for you. I want the address of the lowlife you had attack me."

"Fuck off!" spat the woman from the floor, splayed over Lemoine. I kicked Lemoine savagely in the thigh. He screamed.

"I want the address!" I shouted, viciously. I was not interested in subtlety this evening.

"Fuck off!" the woman shouted. "Are you deaf?"

With my left arm holding her down on top of him, I hit Lemoine with my right fist in the stomach. He screamed again.

"Get off me, you fat bitch!" he shouted at the love of his life.

"Don't call me fat!" With her elbow, she hit him for me.

"The address!" I dragged her off him. With her struggling, it was no mean feat. I pushed her further into the house and hit Lemoine again.

"Stop hitting me!" he screamed. "It's *her* brother, not mine!"

"Address?" He spat out a street name. I frisked him and found his mobile. I removed the sim card and dropped the phone onto his chest.

"Don't hit me again!" he pleaded.

Before I could reply, there was a scream ahead of me. From out of the kitchen, the enraged woman flew at me with a carving knife held out in front. I did a quick sidestep—pushed my right hand against the arm holding the knife, knocking her off balance. I hit her with my left fist—not too hard—right on her ear. She screamed and dramatically fell. I should have hit her again for overacting.

Lemoine screamed, "My leg! My leg! You fat dumb bitch—you've stabbed me in the leg!"

I searched her handbag and found her mobile. I removed her sim card.

She screamed back up at me, "Look what you've done, you fucker!" She had sat back, and was now transfixed on the carving knife sticking out of her lover's thigh. I dropped her phone onto her.

Lemoine was writhing in pain. "Call an ambulance! Call an ambulance!" he screamed.

"How can I?" she screamed back. "He's taken my sim card, you dumb fuck!"

Out on the footpath, I made a phone call. I went back to the doorway and shouted, "Cheer up! The ambulance is on its way!"

I dropped the sim cards to the side of their front door. I walked off quickly, becoming consumed by growing regret. I hate violence towards women—and here I was leaving a house in which I'd just thumped a woman in the ear. It was an ironical regret I was going to have to live with.

I didn't need the house number, only the street name—Vernier—over near Remy's warehouse. The old, carefully restored Renault was parked half on the footpath, half on the street. I looked around. No one was on the street and in all the buildings fronting it, the curtains and blinds were drawn.

I knelt by the front tyre and removed a toothpick from the pocket of my new leather jacket. I slid it into the valve. The air hissed out immediately. I repeated that a further three times. I walked off into the dark, pleased with my night's work.

Chapter 17

There was a knock on my door. My bedside clock showed: 7.12. Climbing out of bed, I crossed to the knock and opened my apartment door. A police badge greeted me.

I thought suddenly, *those idiots—Lemoine and his tart—haven't reported last night's incident to the cops, have they?* The badge lowered to reveal the face of the man who had been waiting in the hospital.

"Good morning," he said. "May I come in?"

"Don't you need a warrant?" I asked, knowing he did, and knowing he'd be entering all the same without one.

"For a neighbourly chat?" he asked. "Don't be silly," he added, attempting to dismiss my concerns. Detective Raphael Legrande walked past me. He pointed to the walls. "When you planning on finishing it?"

"This weekend, if I'm not interrupted," I said pointedly. "If it's not completed, I'll put it down to police interference."

"I won't keep you. May I sit?"

"Sure. Like a coffee?"

"That would be nice." He made it sound as if we were long-lost buddies, catching up on old times.

"Did your mother send you up to check on my well-being?" I asked. "She's very thoughtful that way."

"Something like that." He didn't sit. He followed me into my small kitchen. "I see you've made a shrine to Danielle Hubert."

"It's not a shrine. It's a memorial wall."

"There's a difference?" he asked, as if he really would like to know.

I turned on the tap over the kettle. "Yes, no candle."

He watched me carefully. "Why has my brother been in contact with you?"

"Your mother keeps no secrets from her sons."

"No. She loves us equally. She turns a blind eye to his nefarious activities. I try not to, when they cross into my line of work."

"And your mother doesn't turn a blind eye to your 'wrongful arrests'; 'verballing of suspects'; 'coercion of confessions'; 'remand cell beatings'?"

He said nothing. We stood like that until the old-fashioned kettle—Remy did not deal in anything new, apart from my leather jacket—whistled.

"No milk, eh?" He indicated my shopping list.

"That's old," I explained. "I don't take it down. Next week I'll still need those same items on the list."

He looked again at it. "You go through a packet of toothpicks every week?"

I said nothing. As I opened my fridge door, Raphael asked, "That fifty euro note—sentimental?"

"Yes. It once wasn't, but I think it now is," I explained honestly. Honesty? In front of a cop? I'd better watch myself. Maybe Raphael Legrande's investigative technique was firmly rooted in 'charm'. I poured milk into his coffee.

"No sugar, thank you."

"I wasn't offering any," I quipped. We sat at my small dining table.

"Who's this woman you're looking for?" He asked, not wasting time getting started. "The woman my brother wants you to find," he qualified, as if I had several missing women I was searching for. I said nothing. "We don't have a report of a missing woman in the last three, four weeks."

"I'll trade you information," I finally conceded.

"I'm a detective. It doesn't work like that." He sipped his coffee, keeping an eye on me.

"Wash the cup and close the door on the way out, please." I stood.

He looked at me and smiled. "Okay. I'll trade, but only if you've something worth trading for and it doesn't jeopardise my enquiries."

I considered that. "Her name is Eloise Pittard," I said, sitting opposite him once more. It almost felt as if we were equals.

"That's what *maman* said. So it's her real name?"

"As far as I can make out—I'd say 'yes'."

"Go on," he said looking at me from over the top of the coffee cup.

I posed him a question—I wasn't joining the dots for him as well. "What could possibly link your brother with two very beautiful young women—one dead and one missing?"

He was impressed. "You've seen the naked asses of two exclusively managed women? How did you afford it?" I said nothing. "How long you been here in Nice?" I didn't answer—he knew—he'd told his brother—his brother had told me. Ah, the circles of life.

"I've given you the link—the *fleur-de-lis*. Now, something in return, please. Are there any striking wounds or marks on Danielle's body?"

"In what way 'striking'?" he asked, wanting clarification.

"Out of the ordinary."

He didn't say a word. He held three fingers out and ran them down his side.

"Both sides?" I asked. He nodded. We sat drinking our coffee.

"This missing girl," he began, "has she got the same distinguishing features on her?" I didn't say anything. "Come on. I know you found her in the street—everyone in the building knows that, gossip travels—you're a good Samaritan, not a suspect. Besides, for helping my mother when she had her heart attack, I'd give you until sundown to get out of town before I began hunting you." He laughed. I appreciated his wit and intelligence. The two brothers had not been denied their mother's likeability.

I needed to make clear something for him. "Your brother is not connected to the disappearance and murder of these women."

"I know my brother—he'd never hurt his investments."

"Getting back to Danielle—was she cut? Knifed? Blood spattered?"

"No—just dumped with those scratch marks—no stab wounds."

"And bruising where she'd been tied around the ankles? Tied around the wrists? And bruises under the neck?"

He pursed his lips in thought. "Are you sure you didn't kill her?"

I didn't answer that.

"I'll take your silence as a 'no'," he smiled.

Then Raphael turned on his formal police voice, as if he was explaining to a disbelieving magistrate in a court of law. "The bruising on the neck indicates that Danielle was lifted aloft—pushed up. She'd been held there—we're looking for a strong person. I'd say she's struggled to get free and strangled up there. Pressure marks indicate fingers and thumb. One side of her neck, the right side has deeper bruising than the other. The killer is left-handed."

I took in the information and again felt sorry for the young blonde. It was time to explain to Raphael. "My theory is—Danielle wasn't supposed to have died. She was supposed to have lived and be dumped on a street somewhere, like Eloise. But the killer or killers panicked when she stopped breathing and they dumped her on a tip."

He sat back considering that. "You should be the detective."

"Anything else?" I asked.

He paused, considering what, or if, he was going to say further. "Her vagina had no semen."

"He used a condom."

"No. No evidence of penile entry." I moved my face quizzically. "Yes, very curious. There is however, inside her vagina, deposits of saliva."

"DNA?"

"No match." He leant forward. "You get any hints as to who might have killed her, you let me know. Find Eloise—I won't be looking for her—her disappearance officially doesn't exist. Ask her who did that stuff to her and then we'll know who killed Danielle."

I knew that—I'd joined those dots much earlier.

"Come to me—sidestep my brother. I don't like finding dead women discarded on the town's rubbish tip. And the mayor doesn't like it either—it's a bad look for tourism. The Riviera is about hedonism—the type you do in public, in daylight, not the type you hide in private in the shadows."

He stood and made his way to my doorway. He opened the door and turned. "Thanks for saving my mother. We're even." He left.

I thought, *no semen—because that was on the rear seat of the hire car*. I stopped. I had that bit correct. However it still wasn't quite making sense, for when Milovic 'hired out' his car and wasn't in it, Danielle was still alive. I wondered if greed had got the better of him and he'd hired out his car a third time.

Chapter 18

I waited until Detective Legrande had either left the building or dropped in to farewell his mother. Not that I felt threatened by him, it was just my natural suspicion of police. I try to avoid them at all costs. I'm not one to protest on the street and charge at them with my bare fists and hastily painted placard.

I headed out to a hardware shop several streets over. I bought ten litres of cream paint, a roller and tray, and a brush to cut in with.

I moved the sofa, the table and chairs into the centre of the room, and covered them with an old bed sheet I'd found at Remy's when tidying up that first time. Two hours later, the walls of the living room had their first coat. I stood back admiringly. I left for Claude's for a late morning coffee.

Someone had left the morning newspaper on the counter. I snaffled it and sat outside. All week the story of the Deputy Mayor and his estranged wife had been dragging on through the media starved for local news. Today, desperately trying to keep air in the story, it petered out. They'd published an old photo of the couple 'in happier days'—anything to keep the scandal selling papers.

"Well, well, well," I said cynically to myself. The Deputy Mayor's wife, Felicity, was none other than my Madame Ardoin.

What favours could she possibly owe Pierre Legrande, for her to become part of his poor subterfuge? I clicked my fingers—I knew. She'd hired Danielle through Pierre to be in that out-of-the-way apartment, which Jules and I just happened to drop into with a camera! After the Deputy Mayor had locked the door I bet Danielle, under instruction, had unlocked it. She knew there'd be a photographic team dropping by soon after. That's why she'd kept her head down.

The whole thing smacked of politics and passions and power struggle. I was not going there. Little people, like me, get caught up in their machinations and end up spewed out—like poor Danielle! Maybe I was already caught up in it and didn't know. I hope I'd know when the time came to jump before the axe fell.

I looked at Felicity's photograph again and recalled Jules' assessment of her. 'The wife's a bitch. She needs the cards turned on her.'

During the week, M'sieur Pom told me that the Deputy Mayor had stepped down. For Pierre Deschamps, I'm sure the affair wasn't over. Oh, the sexual one with Danielle was, however the now ex-Deputy Mayor was not old enough to drift off the scene and retire to a farm somewhere to grow lavender. Knowing politicians the world over, I figured he'd be keeping his head down, though only for a while.

For clarification, I needed to run a question by Pierre Legrande. I phoned him.

Pierre Legrande had no idea who Danielle had gone off with. There'd been no 'booking' for her the night she was killed. Also, there'd been no booking for Eloise the night she was dumped on my doorstep. They'd gone off with someone different to their normal clientelè. Someone who appeared to be exciting, out of the ordinary—even famous?

As a child, my mother used to say, "I don't mind who you play with, just let me know where you'll always be." These two girls had not heeded my mother's advice.

I wondered if Danielle had said anything to me, sitting on the sofa, sipping her Bloody Mary. I tried recalling, finally admitting she hadn't. I wondered if she'd said anything that night, or the night previously in the bedroom. It was time to ask the writer how much he knew about her.

I walked down towards the sea, returning to the hired apartment of the writer Philip J. Phillips. I rang the intercom downstairs.

"Yes?"

"Philip J. Phillips, please."

"Sorry—never heard of him. We only arrived this morning."

"Okay—thank you."

*

It was late afternoon when I approached the marina at Cannes. I was pleased to see Milovic's hire car parked in its usual spot. I came up behind him and tickled him under his armpits. I sprang back as he jumped around. "Hey!!!" we both shouted at once.

"Milos tells me you made a sorry sight during the week," Milovic said, reminding me. I wished he hadn't. "Getting over some woman?"

"Of course—you know me too well, Milovic. Are you driving the Hollywood lovers around today?"

"Of course." He felt my leather jacket. "Nice, very nice," he added, pushing forward his lower lip in appreciation.

I became serious for a moment. "Mate—I know you let him and his pal drive your car—you told me, remember?" He nodded. "Did they drive the car a third time?"

Enough slivovitz had passed under our twin bridges, for him not to ask why I wished to know.

"A third time? No. However, they may have. I would not know. Ulna was ill. I only drove days last week, not nights. It's too dangerous to shag your wife in the back seat during daylight—everyone can see!" He laughed.

I nodded, not entirely disappointed, as my thoughts still held water. Someone else could have let that muscled assistant drive the car.

"See you Saturday night?" he asked me.

"I'll be there." I patted him on the upper arm and headed down to *The Blue Dahlia*.

The skipper was on the stern of the boat. He saw me approaching and turned inside—his bandy legs disappearing. That vision was replaced with the stare of Ms Walton. She eyed me walking towards her. If she had been Francine, I'd swear she was checking out my 'credentials', studying every step I made coming towards her, while planning on putting them to use later in the evening. I lurched back to reality. *If she changed that face mask, cracking it with a smile, she'd be a bit of a catch*, I thought. *Mind you, the catch would not be an edible sea bass, more likely a stingray.*

She pointed. "You're not carrying anything. What are you delivering?"

"Today I'm not a courier—I'm doing market research." I laughed. She didn't. "I'm only kidding. I was wondering if I could ask you a few questions."

"Market research—a step up in life—I wondered how you'd managed to be wearing such a quality leather jacket. You almost look presentable." What was with this woman? Did she degrade every man or had she taken a particular shining to me? She pointed at my wristwatch. I wondered if she was going to accuse me of stealing it. She surprised me, asking, "What's the time?"

I checked it. "Nearly five. Seven before."

"In seven minutes, I finish work for the day. Then I'll answer anything you like. Come on board." I did. She pointed to the bench seat I'd occupied that first time. "Sit there."

She went down to the cabins below. I moved so I could get a look at the activity I could hear happening up on deck.

I eased my way to the ladder, lifting myself noiselessly up a rung. On the deck above, Kempenski was lying back in the sun, the deck chair supporting his heavy ass, nearly touching the deck. He was smoking a fat cigar, trying to blow rings in the air, living his clichéd dream.

Calvin deMarko was effortlessly pumping iron. He was bare-chested and covered in perspiration—an image, screaming fans all over the world would have paid money for. I noted he had on tight swim shorts. Was he gay after all? He had a look of a man not needing to conceal who he was.

Pumping iron with Calvin was his assistant Beau. He didn't need to hide anything. There's something a little disconcerting watching all those oiled muscles in arms and legs, gathered around the groin area by a wrestler's black jockstrap. I noticed Beau had eyes only for his old high school buddy.

Belinda Swann was doing some sort of yoga exercise, clad in white exercise pants and sports bra, her entire collection of unmentionables thrust in my direction. I would now never need to buy a cinema ticket to any of her future films as I had now seen every notable performance she was capable of delivering.

She stopped. She crossed to her husband and rubbed his arm muscles and jokingly said something. Kempenski removed the cigar and laughed out loud raucously—it was the sound I'd heard on my first visit. Beau laughed as well, though unlike Kempenski's naturalness, his seemed forced. I got the feeling that perhaps he didn't like Belinda touching Calvin on his arm muscles. Perhaps he felt that was reserved for him.

Calvin kept pumping. Then Belinda said something admonishing Beau and laughed. She grabbed Calvin, however this time on his nuts and he jumped sky high with surprise.

Calvin told her not to do that again while he was pumping iron! What a clown. I'd have let her continue all afternoon and long into the night.

"Ready?"

I snapped out of my fanciful reverie. I turned. Ms Walton had applied makeup and lipstick, appearing to be a different woman—softer. Perhaps she was human after all.

She eased me aside and shouted up the stairs. "Mister Kempenski! *Au revoir*!"

Kempenski shouted something back, which was lost on me—maybe his accent, maybe the breeze carried away his words, maybe I was still taken by the altered vision of his production assistant.

She stepped off the boat onto the pier. I followed.

"Fridays at five—I quit. After a whole week couped up on *The Blue Dahlia*, I need to get on land and find a bar. Care to join me?"

"Me?"

"Sure. I'm also sick of drinking alone and sick of men trying to pick me up. They'll take one look at you and stay away. They'll figure I'm a nurse still on duty." She laughed! She laughed at me! What is with this woman?

"Come on." She took hold of my arm and walked me down the pier between all the moored yachts.

"What makes you think I haven't anything important on?" I stopped and released her arm. "What makes you think I *want* to? What is it with you, lady?"

"Lady? I'm no lady!" She was now laughingly deriding herself! She noted my puzzlement and seriously said, "Thank God—a man with spirit, not the type to be pushed around. I kind of hoped you'd be worth knowing." I looked at her not comprehending. "Okay—I'm sorry," she confessed. "Would you care to join me? There's a quiet bar I know—up town."

I was not used to this, this...What other offers did I have? It was Friday evening and Francine sure wasn't going to call.

Mary-Anne stood there in the summer evening light, and the moment after she undid her ponytail and tossed out her hair, I said, "Nothing on—lead the way."

Up near the car park, Milovic saw us coming. He surreptitiously dropped his cigarette and turned his shoe on it. He gave no sign of recognition and I returned the non-gesture. Those of us in the servant class know the rules when we see another one of us is working.

We also know when one of us is punching above our weight. Mary-Anne Walton was so far above mine, I thought about phoning Remy to see if he could sell me a second-hand step ladder.

Chapter 19

She led me away from the parked cars, away from the strolling tourists on the foreshore and up towards the old area—le Suquet. As we climbed the winding cobbled lane, she wove her arm through mine again. "Do you mind?" she asked.

"No." I tried to act calmly, as if this gesture of hers was an everyday event for me. Unbelievably, from the first step, we walked side by side in sync, as if seated, moving effortlessly forward, on a giant swing in a children's playground. I wondered where the other woman had gone—and which one was real. Perhaps spending a life around actors, she'd learnt how to be one. Was this woman on my arm the performance? Or was that the woman she'd left back on board *The Blue Dahlia*?

She led me into a bar. She waved to the waiter who smiled back. She'd been here before—probably immediately after work every Friday night she'd been in Cannes. The barman gave me an extended look of assessment.

"Sit at a table or at the bar?" she asked.

I offered her all my worldly advice. "Ladies don't like sitting at the bar."

"Then let's sit at the bar." She took my hand and led me down the far end, around the return of the counter. The barman placed two coasters in front of us, though he made a point of not placing mine directly in front of me. I adjusted my sitting position several times on the stool. She noted that I seemed to be uncomfortable. I wasn't—I just needed to get my foot on the rung which was a little higher from the ground than I expected.

"We can sit at a table, if you wish."

"No, no—this is fine." I smiled and looked about the bar. It had a chic-grunge design. The old motorbike mounted on the wall behind the counter dominated the room's visuals. The clientele was like her. I couldn't get a handle on any of them. I decided they were rich people, enjoying not appearing to be rich.

"Can I let you in on secret?" Before I could tell her she could, she went on. "I love to drink beer. But here in Cannes and the crowd I mix with, well beer's hardly *de riguer*. After a time, all that bubbly and coloured icy stuff only makes you drunk. Beer aids *conversation*!"

Aids bullshit, I thought, employing my Aussie insight.

"Two beers please, Paul." She leant into me. "Paul's worried by your presence. You're the first man to ever accompany me in here."

"Perhaps you could tell him I'm a hot Hollywood producer."

She eased back looking at me. "No—even a barman hoping for a tip would not believe that. However that jacket suits you—black matches your eyes—after you've lost a fight." She laughed again. She added, "You do drink beer, don't you?"

"Oh yes." I tried not to appear too eager. "Have you ever tasted Australian beer?"

"No, never. You've been there?"

"Been there? I was born here in France and I grew up in Australia—nearly forty years' worth of growing up."

She suddenly switched from French to English. "You're an Aussie!"

I was taken aback—by the sudden language shift and by her accent.

"You're…Manhattan?…The Bronx?"

"New Jersey." And then she said something to me in the broadest New Jersey accent she could muster.

"What did you just say, mate?" I asked in the broadest Australian accent I possessed.

We both eased ourselves back, as far as we could from each other without falling from our stools, and looked in mock amazement.

I said again, in French, "What did you just say?"

She laughed. "We both speak English, but we cannot understand each other!"

"Imagine if a Scotsman was with us!" I joked.

Speaking English seemed to have changed her. Her eyes were alight. She was genuinely at ease and happily so. I admit I was as well.

By the end of the hour, and draining our third beer, we were speaking in sentences that switched liberally between French and English.

She ordered food and a large pile of salad appeared. With two awkwardly designed utensils, she lifted food onto her small plate. I followed suit. I noted during the course of the next fifteen minutes that she had a peculiarity. Whereas

I, and I assumed most people, eat different vegetables and fruits of the salad as one, she ate all the tomato first, then all the lettuce, then all the other things.

"Here," she said, lifting the serving spoon towards me, "I don't like mushrooms." Without waiting for a reply, she dropped them onto my plate.

Over two hours later, I reached for my wallet.

"No," she said, finding in her purse a credit card and handing it to the barman. "This evening is on Mister Kempenski." I didn't object.

"Walk you home?" I asked as we leant against each other in the doorway of the bar, trying to stay upright.

"Walk me home? How old-fashioned."

"I'm an old-fashioned kind of guy." She laughed—I laughed with her. With the amount of beer we'd consumed, we'd have laughed at anything. We staggered towards the water. I was thankful it was downhill, though I did remind myself that the return journey wasn't.

Milovic was not standing by his hire car, because the hire car was not there. The Hollywood trio had left the boat and were now somewhere on dry land.

At the stern of *The Blue Dahlia*, she stopped and I asked her, "That name—I've heard it before."

"What name?"

"Your boat."

"Oh. It's from a famous black and white detective film. Alan Ladd and Gene Tierney—no—Veronica Lake. I think Raymond Chandler meant something when he chose that as a title. It's somehow ironic or carries some deeper meaning."

"How so?"

"All Dahlia colours attract pollination—except blue. So it's pointless to have a blue dahlia." I nodded as if I understood. "So technically it serves no true purpose. I guess it doesn't exist." She laughed. "I'd never thought about it. A bit like our business deals, the basis a film is made on. We don't leave behind us monuments or buildings, just flickering images." She snuffled a 'Huh!' "Sand not rock," she said, suddenly miles away. She'd lost me. She flicked back to now. "Weren't you wanting to ask me some questions?"

I'd forgotten. I'd been in Nice for—what?—four or five months and tonight was the first time I'd spent in the company of a beautiful woman in a bar, eating, drinking, conversing in two languages and being captivated by the moment. Yes, she was beautiful. Sometime during the evening, I'd realised that.

"That blonde," I started, though I didn't go on. I'd drunk more than I thought.

"There are a lot of blondes, Dougay."

"That blonde—at the writer's apartment." Eventually I'd get it all out.

"Why be interested in a blonde when you have me?" I looked at her. She laughed. She was back to her best kidding self. She consoled me, whispering, as if warning me, "Dougay, she's out of your league."

I tried to explain. She spoke over me.

"Look around—we are on *The French Riviera*. Try and imagine the total worth of only these boats you can see. Here, the richest people in the world live, work and play. And some of them like to have exceedingly beautiful women hanging around them. And they pay for that to happen. Call it set dressing; visual enhancement; whatever. And if some want to 'get to know each other a bit better'—as the cliché goes—then…it's a fact of life here."

I said bluntly, "That screenwriter couldn't have afforded this blonde I saw him with."

"She was a gift—an 'advance reward' to make Mister Phillips, the Oscar nominated screenwriter, finish the screenplay on time," she said with a lace of sarcasm. I gathered she didn't much respect the work of Philip J. Phillips. Then again, I remembered what she'd done to his script with her red pencil!

"Mister Kempenski needed the screenplay completed. He wanted Calvin deMarko to read it—not that he's a very fast reader, he's probably thrown by words of three syllables. Mister Kempenski desperately wanted deMarko's signature on a contract—simple as that."

"Where'd he find her?"

"Who?"

"The blonde."

"Why are you interested?"

"Please—humour me," I stated seriously.

"I don't know—washed up on some beach?" She saw I didn't believe her. "Why are you so interested? I know you're not wanting to bed her, when you can have me." She laughed at me again. She was beginning to morph back into the other woman.

"The blonde is Danielle Hubert. She's gone missing." I lied—a little. Ms Walton did not correct me. She did not know that Danielle was no longer with us. "I've been asked to try and find her whereabouts."

"What? You're an undercover flic?"

"No, no, no. Someone—an old boss of hers—someone like that, has asked me."

Ms Walton carefully considered what she'd say and how she'd say it.

"Last week, sometime, there was a party, on board here. Mister Kempenski had several potential investors—American men who'd flown over. He gave them a good time, hoping they'd invest in this next project. He'd been hinting that Calvin deMarko was interested and to show that, he had Calvin here, in person—probably paying him for the live performance. The blonde was at the party."

"And Calvin's wife? They seem very close."

"Oh, she was here. She never lets Calvin out of her sight. She also didn't let some of the girls out of her sight as well." I got the impression Ms Walton was not a fan of either of them. "Don't tell anyone—the press must never know—but Belinda Swann lays both ways in bed."

"Both ways?" I asked, trying not to make out I understood, hoping she'd continue.

"Men and women! Though the only man she's interested in is Calvin. When it comes to women, she likes plenty of them, as long as they stay nameless. Why am I telling you this?"

"Because I'm handsome."

She laughed. She placed her open hand against my cheek, as if comforting a child. "You're excellent company, you know that." Was she dismissing me?

"When I was first here," I said, not wishing to let go of the moment, nor my inquisitive tack, "I remember a stunning red head—had a tattoo on her ass."

"Next you'll be asking to see mine." She laughed. "The girls come through a service. Kempenski makes use of it. 'Milady'. They're not in the phone book. Those girls have that—tattoo. Someone's idea of cuteness, I guess."

"Milady?"

"*Fleur-de-lis*—Milady—get it?"

"No." I was not playing dumb.

She looked at me. "Why are interesting men so…" She left it dangling.

"First you need *The Blue Dahlia* explained and now this. All you want is historical explanation from me, and I thought you wanted to get into my knickers! Good night."

She turned to go. "Ms Walton? Mary-Anne?" She stopped. "Milady?" I stressed.

She turned back and smiled. "Alexandre Dumas. *The Three Musketeers*. Milday de Winter has a fleur-de-lis branded on her shoulder. She's part of the aristocracy, but has a secret. She'd been a whore in her youth."

I said, "So—*The Blue Dahlia* and 'Milady de Winter'— both not what they seemed to be."

"Bravo!" She gave me her hand. I shook it. I was not getting a goodnight kiss.

Chapter 20

I passed the spot where Milovic always seemed to park and was reminded of a fear I'd had earlier. I rang Pierre Legrande. It was after 'business hours'. I didn't care.

"A simple question—is your redhead *still* okay?" There was no reply. "Is she *still* safe?" Another pause. What is it with 'business men'? Why can't they give an unreserved answer? "My question is not loaded," I said, a terseness in my voice. Perhaps he picked up on that, who knows what drives these types.

"Yes, she's safe," he finally admitted.

"Do you know where she is tonight?" There was a pause.

A female voice said, "Hello. Yes, I'm safe."

Pierre then hung up. It had been like pulling teeth from a reluctant teenager. I tried not to think about the redhead being with her boss at night.

I then phoned Jules. He answered. "Do you know what time this is?" He was acting upset. "You're still alive then."

"I need a confirmation."

"Go to mass on Sunday." He hung up. I redialled. He answered again, still laughing.

"All those girls with those decorated asses—do they go under the name of 'Milady'?"

"Don't call me again!" He hung up. He wasn't laughing any longer.

It was then I noticed I had a text message. It had been sent three hours before, while I was in the bar with Mary-Anne. It was from Francine. It read: Café *de Paris. 10.30.* I looked at my watch. It was well past that time and I was still in Cannes waiting for the late train.

I headed to Francine's apartment when I left Gare de Nice. Several blocks over I gave the idea away. What was the point? Francine would only chew me out, and then deny me entry. Tonight, I hadn't escorted her home from the bar and to tell the truth I wasn't concerned. I'd had a far more fulfilling evening. What could Francine only offer me late on a Friday night? Sex.

I recommenced walking towards her apartment. After a short burst, each step became more reluctant. She was using me as her plaything—though hardly a toy boy. I hadn't been complaining about that, for I needed to retain the job of running her errands, and I loved being in her bed. Don't get me wrong, I really thought I'd loved the woman—I honestly thought I wanted to move that relationship to another level. Clearly, a level she had no desire to join me at. I admitted to myself that I'd blown that relationship on Wednesday night. There was no going back.

I stopped walking again. I had no idea where I was. Sick of walking, I hailed a cab! I went home to bed. M'sieur Pom was not at his desk in the foyer. It was even too late for him.

*

I woke and felt like cereal for breakfast. Opening the fridge, I smelt the milk. It was off. I poured it down the sink. As I picked up my wallet, I had a nasty feeling. Last night, I had handed the taxi driver a ten and a twenty. He'd kept the change. I was too drunk or too tired or too bound up in my own thoughts to have fully noticed. My wallet was empty.

I remembered Eloise's fifty euro pinned to the notice board. I didn't want to take it down. Maybe I would after I found her—however, not now. I walked away from it. Short-term survival got the better of me. I went and removed the pin, and immediately felt bad about doing so. I held it up and said, "No, Eloise—I'll hold onto you a little longer."

Sometimes some things just fall into your lap. In this case, they'd always been there and I was too blind to see. Around the edge of the note was a series of numbers written in a small delicate hand.

I dialled the number. I said who I was. The female voice at the other end asked, "What kept you?"

*

On Rue Beethoven, opposite Place Mozart, I waited in the sunshine for Remy's truck. I waved to Madame Legrande sitting, enjoying the weather, on her favourite bench. She waved back and wished me well. *Tell your sons, that*, I thought.

I heard the truck before I saw it. Remy pulled up and I got in. As I adjusted the poorly fitting seatbelt, he asked, "Today, are we the good guys or the bad guys?"

"Good guys. We're on a rescue mission—a mission of discovery."

"We're diving for the wreck of the Hesperus?" He laughed because I didn't understand. "It's a famous poem or story or something." Between Ms Walton and him, I felt I was going to need a crash course in literary, filmic and cultural references.

We took the coastal road east from Nice, the morning sun shining on my right arm resting on the open window. I loved the summer breeze blowing in my face, like a tradesman's faithful dog, accompanying his master. Above the beach at Villefranche-sur-Mer, I wondered if I'd ever swim there again with Francine. I remembered her leaving the water and me admiringly thinking, *I could be happy with this woman*. Who was I kidding? I knew I wouldn't swim there with her again.

Further along, Remy turned left and immediately we started climbing. On every sharp bend, and there were many of them, I looked back out my window, watching the Mediterranean drop further and further away.

We waited for tourist coaches to manoeuvre themselves into the parking bays at Eze and then continued on a little further. Remy stopped and set up his portable GPS. I typed in the address. We set off again.

"You have reached your destination," said the machine.

Ahead was a dirt track leading through a dilapidated gate to an old stone farmhouse, some trees irregularly spaced either side of it. The truck bounced carefully down the path.

"Don't get too close," I warned. "I don't want to spook them. Stop here."

Remy did. I climbed out and took off my leather jacket. I placed it on the front seat I'd just vacated. Remy looked at me puzzled.

"Just in case she doesn't recognise me in quality clothing," I explained.

Remy scoffed. We walked slowly together towards the farmhouse. The door opened. A woman appeared on the porch.

"Stay there!" she called out. From her side, she half lifted a shotgun. She stood staring at us.

"You!" she pointed. "I know you. You're…Remy Didion. I saw your last fight. According to the papers, you broke your hand, which is why you lost."

Remy said nothing. I spoke to him out the corner of my mouth.

"Go on—answer her—before she decides to shoot us." Remy said nothing. "I don't care if you end up dead, but I kind of like the breathing pattern I've been employing for the past forty years." He didn't move. "She probably had money on that fight and she lost her life savings." He didn't move or speak. I hissed out of the side of my mouth, "Placate her loss!"

Remy finally called out, "That's correct, Madame." He raised his right hand and shook it. "On cold nights—I still feel the punch that did it."

"Come forward—ten paces." We did so.

"Stop there!" We did so.

"Turn around!" We did so. I hoped she wasn't going to shoot us in the back.

A young woman stood over there, under a tree. I called out, "Hello, Eloise."

Chapter 21

After she'd put down the shotgun, the woman insisted we have coffee. She went inside with Eloise to make it and Remy and I sat on the old wooden bench off the porch, on a small paved area.

"One could be miles and miles away from all care up here." I settled back breathing in the fresh air.

"Yes," said Remy. "It's very quiet."

We both sat and waited. The elder woman returned with a tray and Eloise carried some biscuits.

"Homemade," she said. "Angelie is the best cook."

We sipped our coffee and chewed the biscuits. Eloise was correct—Angelie was a superb baker.

Eventually, Angelie said, "Remy, come with me. I want to show you my estate." She thumped him on the arm. "Come on, I said."

"You hit me, Madame!" exclaimed a shocked Remy.

"I've wanted to do that ever since I lost a hundred euro on you all those years back."

I'd been right. Remy followed her. I waited for Eloise to speak. I settled back as I was in no hurry.

"I was scared," she began to explain, hesitatingly. "I'd been slapped around before. I guess in my game, who hasn't been?"

"It still doesn't make it acceptable," I consoled her, not knowing where the conversation was headed.

"When I woke at your apartment, I checked my purse. You hadn't stolen from me. You hadn't tried to drag me to your bed. I couldn't believe I'd been saved by an honourable man—a knight in shining armour. I wanted to thank you. I left you the money in your shirt pocket. Then I thought that if you took the time to care about me, then you might like to know what became of me. I removed the note and wrote down my mobile number. I laughed at you, you know. You were snoring."

"I don't snore!"

"Yes, you do—like a foghorn out on a misty sea." She laughed. I was pleased she hadn't lost that ability.

"I called Angelie. She was the only person I knew I could rely on."

"Pierre? You didn't think of calling him?"

She looked at me. "How much do you know?" she asked, concerned.

"Some." That was all I was prepared to admit to just now. I didn't wish to influence her story—I needed her truth, not the truth she thought I wanted to hear.

"No. I hadn't told Pierre about the job at all. The offer was too good to refuse and it didn't come through Pierre. I was moonlighting. I guess I became blasé about the protection provided by being under his wing. I learnt my lesson the hard way."

I let her gather her thoughts. Someway off I saw Angelie strolling with Remy. He was gesticulating, probably describing in minute detail how he lost the fight and apologising to her for her losing her money.

"Angelie is a friend. She's also a client." I looked at Eloise. "*Was* a client," she corrected. "You'd never know she was once a high flyer—the world of international banking. A brain that can calculate amounts of figures I did not know existed."

I understood perfectly what she meant. I knew what twenty euro could buy me. I had no idea what twenty million euro could.

"Yes, I go with men and women. That's no big deal—these days—is it? Angelie never slapped me about."

I sipped the remnants of my coffee. "That's cold," she said. "I'll get you a fresh cup."

She went inside. The sun was nearly overhead now, and it wasn't hot. Up here in the mountains I guess it was always cool. I went back to the truck and put on my leather jacket. As I returned, Eloise was placing the cup before me.

"Angelie wants me to stay. Or if I go back, to retire here as soon as I can—to get out of the business—and settle with her. Raise goats or something."

I could understand her desire for a quiet life. And I could understand the wish of the older woman to take on the role of protector.

"Eloise, your facial bruising has healed. What are your sides like?"

She leant forward and lifted her top to show me one side of herself. There were three long half healed scabs, running down her body. "They'll mend," she admitted. She pulled down her top. "This—this attack really scared me."

"I can imagine." I did not know when the time would be right to ask her. I waited.

Eloise noticed. "What is it?"

"Have you heard about Danielle? Danielle Hubert?"

"No."

"She's been found dead." Eloise said nothing. She grew distant, I guess reflecting on the times she and Danielle had spent together. I didn't want to say how I knew Danielle, though I knew Eloise would want to know. "I met Danielle, delivering a film script to *The Blue Dahlia*."

She smiled, "Good parties onboard *The Blue Dahlia*. Good money was made there."

"You haven't heard any news up here?"

"Angelie listens to the stock market everyday—but local stuff—not really."

"Danielle was found strangled." Eloise's hand went unthinkingly to her own throat. "She had similar side scars as you have."

Eloise sat back in her chair and murmured or groaned or whatever guttural sound you make when deep realisation hits you.

"I'm sorry, Eloise, I have to know what happened. Pierre wants to know and so does his brother, the detective."

"Were you followed here?" She was suddenly alert.

"No. And they're not going to hurt you. They're not *interested* in hurting you. The detective wants the case solved and Pierre wants to know if you're safe, and I guess, if you're going back to him. They both want to know who killed Danielle." I indicated her side. "Please tell me—take your time."

She rose and moved off the paved area and stood on the grass, though she didn't feel comfortable there. She moved over to the tree, the one she was standing beneath when I first saw her. I got up to follow her. She heard my chair scrape and turned. She held up her hand. I sat back down and waited for her to return. I had my theories, though not the detail. I needed her to tell me so I could be absolutely sure.

She went inside and returned with a tall glass of water. She sipped and coughed, clearing her throat.

"I waited on a street corner—prearranged. A car pulled up and I got into the back. That was no big deal—I'm very used to being chauffeured. A few minutes later, it stopped. The driver got out and a new driver climbed in. A woman opened the rear door and climbed in next to me. She was hungry. Before she'd settled, she had her hand up my dress and was trying to kiss my mouth. Her fingers were starving.

"I pushed her away a little. I reminded her of the deal. 'Money up front,' I said.

"The car turned into a basement parking area behind this unlit building. The driver stopped the car and tossed over his shoulder a wad of notes. In a clip! I'd never seen that before. I didn't care. I could tell the amount was correct—it felt like three thousand.

"The woman ripped down my G-string, as I was putting the money in my purse. She began kissing me. It wasn't her first time—she'd done this many times—and she knew what she was doing. I confess I started to get—involved. I thought for sure the driver was in front jerking himself off.

"But no, the rear door opened and he climbed in. 'Pull down my pants, bitch! Pull 'em down!' I did as I was told and all the while the woman is sucking the life out of me and when his pants are down, she reaches across and grabs his cock, tugging him ferociously, and says, 'How much do you love me baby?' He's crying out—in agony or ecstasy? I couldn't say. Then he just unloaded—all over the rear seat.

"They'd done this before because they calmed down and took me from the car into the basement. He led the way, but she couldn't let me go. She half-carried me. Inside they tossed me onto the bed and she removed all my clothing and hers and climbed onto me. She was very, very excited. Then I felt the rope go around my ankles and before I could move, they were wrenched tight. I screamed but she was kissing me and hardly any sound got out. I tried to struggle but she was strong. Not heavy, not fat, just strong. She lifted herself from her waist up and pushed down on my shoulders, her other hand over my mouth. The driver took an arm and bound another rope around my wrist. If I thought she was strong, he was far stronger. He found my other arm and bound my wrists together. He stuffed a rag between my teeth. I'm not a fan of that—I tend to gag—suffocate easily. 'Lay still, bitch!' He punched me in the face. More than once. I lay still—I was scared, very scared.

"The woman had her pleasure with me. If I hadn't been tied up, I confess I would have genuinely enjoyed her. It was like having the tables turned. You know, an expert being in the hands of another expert.

"Then the driver suddenly shouts, 'You bitch! How dare you fuck my wife!' He rushed me. He grabbed me by the throat and thumped my head up and down. I clenched my teeth around the rag. I didn't want to bite my tongue. He untied my wrists and ankles, ripping at the knots. Then effortlessly he lifted me into the air, suspended up there by one hand. He shook me like I was a rag doll!

"The woman was playing with his cock—though why I don't know as he'd lost his load outside—saying 'This, what you want, baby?' I started to pass out. My nostrils were fighting for air. He held me there and ripped out the gag. As if on cue I screamed. The woman had stabbed the nails of both her hands into both sides of me and ripped them savagely down. I howled! 'Love that, bitch?' she gloated.

"He held me up there like a trophy he'd won at a sporting event. Then he let me fall. I was nearly unconscious. He slapped my face several times, trying to bring me around, but I couldn't open my eyes. Did they panic—or was this what they'd planned? I have no idea. The woman dressed me and they bundled me back in the car. That's all I remember. I passed out. Did they rape me in the car? I don't know.

"I remember the car moving. I was drifting in and out. The car stopped and the driver tossed over a travel rug. The woman said, 'How much did you blow, baby? It's everywhere—I can't clean it all up.' 'Toss it,' he said. She opened the rear door and did. Then the car drove off for a while. It slowed and the woman kicked me out like a piece of garbage onto the footpath. The impact hurt like hell. I don't even think I had enough life in me to cry out."

I felt devastated for her—our shared silence commentary enough. After a time, I tried to gently break the awkward silence. "And the next thing you knew your hero had arrived and saved you."

She managed a suppressed laugh.

"One final thing, Eloise—do you know who they were?"

Chapter 22

Remy drove back from Eze by the inland road, the route the bus takes. How could such depravity happen down there in a city which, from above, always looked so inviting, so fun loving, so safe?

"She's an interesting woman," said Remy.

I looked sideways across to him as he drove, his eyes firmly on the road ahead. "Which one?" I asked.

"The aunt."

"The aunt? She told you that?"

"Yes. She told me a lot of things. I wonder if I should give her a call sometime—drive back there with an excellent Bordeaux." I didn't say a word. "I really enjoyed walking about her farm talking with her. Though if you're ever up here late at night, be careful wandering around the place."

"Why would I want to?" I asked.

Remy was in a talkative mood—meeting Eloise's 'aunt' had loosened his tongue.

"She showed me a unique geological feature towards the back of the property. Holes—you know—a deep sinkhole thing."

"A fissure?"

"Yes, that's it. Unlike you, she's very astute."

"Astute? You're a second-hand furniture dealer—when did you start admiring 'astuteness'?"

"I wasn't always a dealer."

"No, you were a pugilist."

"Maybe I like meeting my old fans," he conceded.

"She lost money on you!"

"A hundred euro—I could easily give it back to her."

"I hate to toss a bucket of cold water over your plans of seduction, Remy, but she's a lesbian." He glanced furtively sideways, then back to the road. "And she's not an aunt to Eloise." He glanced back again not believing a woman could ever lie to him. "She's her lover."

Five minutes on, after consideration, Remy said, "You string me along sometimes, Dougay."

As we'd been driving carefully out of the farm's driveway, I'd phoned Pierre and told him to meet me at his mother's place in an hour and to make sure his brother was there as well.

Remy dropped me off in front of my apartment block. Madame Legrande was sitting in the park with both her sons. Upon seeing me, they left her and came over. M'sieur Pom watched them escort me through the foyer. He seemed concerned. Raphael opened her apartment door. Inside, the three of us sat.

"Eloise is safe and on the mend," I said. "She'll be back—in two or three weeks. You can't have her working for you until she's in perfect shape, anyway, can you? So patience will be required." Pierre did not answer. "She's still shaken by her experience and she's embarrassed for moonlighting. It appears you really are concerned for and really do look after the women who work for you."

"I didn't send you to get a character reference for me."

I ignored Pierre. I looked at Raphael. "The couple who attacked Eloise is the same couple who killed Danielle."

"Will Eloise be able to identify them?" asked the detective.

"Oh, don't worry about that. She knows who they are. So, brothers Legrande, the saliva in Danielle's vagina, and the scratch marks down both sides of each woman, belongs to Belinda Swann; and Danielle's killer is her husband, Calvin deMarko."

There was silence. Unhurried, Pierre asked, "The movie couple? Americans?"

"Yes." The room returned to silence. The two brothers sat there. They didn't exchange glances. They didn't move.

I went on. "It wasn't the first time they'd performed such perverted acts, though Danielle's death was probably not planned. Some men simply do not know the strength they possess when fully aroused—lust and anger is a lethal combination. Check with police forces in the different American states—or perhaps the FBI. There may be other similar cases of sexual abuse over there."

Still there was no response.

"Well? What do you intend doing about it, detective?" I was becoming concerned at his lack of interest.

"This will cause a stir—quite a stir," he began, trying to find the words, as if he was on a witness stand in a court of law. "My superiors…"

"Oh, great!" I interjected. "A young woman is dead and you're worried about what your superiors are going to do with the international furore?"

"I didn't quite say—"

"You don't have to," I said dismissively. I turned to his elder brother. "What about you, Pierre?"

He sat there. Then he meekly offered, "My brother is the policeman, not I."

"What a pair of jumped-up wankers you two are!" There was no response from them. "Big men of Nice?" I spat out. "Why do the little people shit themselves in *your* presence? I've had enough of you two—*brothers!* Stradling either side of the law? You two couldn't straddle a baby's bath." I stood. "Both of you are a disgrace. Fuck off out of my life!"

I walked away, angrily. As I slammed the door, to Madame Legrande's apartment, I shouted to Pierre, "You can keep your money!" I stormed past M'sieur Pom behind his desk in the foyer. I didn't wave to Madame Legrande in Place Mozart. I headed up hill to Gare de Nice, my anger transferring into the weight of my footsteps.

*

I took the train to Cannes. I didn't know what I was going to do once I got there. It just seemed wrong, inconceivable, that there was so much inaction on the part of the brothers Legrande, now they knew who were responsible for the assault on Eloise Pittard and the death of Danielle Hubert. What could I do—a no one—officially and unofficially about that?

Sitting in the crowded carriage, I stewed. I believe in justice and justice was…

Pierre Legrande, once desperate to find out who'd murdered his 'girl', was uninterested.

Detective Raphael Legrande couldn't or wouldn't act.

Danielle no doubt had serviced too many people in high positions on the Riviera for the case to go any further. It was becoming a cold case, so much so, I could feel the authorities tossing ice onto it.

The 'law' and the 'lawless' of Nice had shelved the idea of justice for her.

On the train, the motion's constant rhythm brought Danielle to my mind. I saw her sitting back on that sofa in the apartment of Philip J. Phillips, putting down her Bloody Mary, beckoning me with her finger, turning over and showing me her tattooed ass and laughing. Laughing with pleasure at her arousal or laughing with disdain at mine? I wondered what I could have done to have saved her. Twenty-twenty hindsight is a wonderful thing. It gives you understanding and puts your inaction into perspective. It left me with a heightened sense of uselessness.

I wasn't a hit man and I wasn't a policeman, however I felt that Hollywood's glamour couple needed exposing and needed some sort of retribution, even if it was the only kind I could administer. I was angry and that irrational anger would not abate.

I needed to hit someone—and that someone was the murdering Calvin deMarko—muscles or no muscles. A well-delivered straight left to the chin followed by a swift kick to his nuts would never be enough.

After I'd dispensed my meagre punishment, I intended grabbing his bitch of a wife by the throat and tossing her overboard. I hoped she couldn't swim.

I jumped with a start as the train's doors started to close. I ran between them. One door caught me on the shoulder. I stumbled onto the platform, keeping my feet.

Milovic, impeccably dressed as per his station, stood by his hire car, in almost the exact spot I'd first found him. I waved fleetingly. He nodded once in smiling recognition.

"So, my favourite drinking companion." He was pleased to see me again. "Is tonight still on?"

I didn't have pleasant chit-chat in me. "Same clients?" I asked, pointing to the car, to him and down to the marina.

"Oh yes." He patted the chest of his jacket. "Call by Vlatava-Elbe tonight and the slivovitz is on me. I'll be there from five."

"Finishing work early today?"

"Yes. I take Cal and Bel to the airport." He looked at his watch. "Soon. Then I head home."

Cal? And Bel? Milovic had been well and truly rewarded.

I stood on the walkway between the yachts, facing the stern of *The Blue Dahlia*. Matty was there coiling rope. He looked up when I called his name.

"Hey," he said, welcomingly. Obviously, he didn't know my intentions. Nor had he read the fire in my eyes.

"Cal on board?" I asked nonchalantly.

"Sure. Step on."

I did and walked past him, my eyes searching, trying to see where Calvin deMarko was.

Matty thumped me in the left kidney. I lurched forward and before I could right myself, he bundled me in his arms and tossed me down towards the cabins below. I started to get to my feet, my kidney throbbing. He sent his right hand into my solar plexus. I fell back. A cabin door opened behind me and he lifted me up with both arms and effortlessly dragged me onto the bunk.

He'd already placed ropes inside the cabin. He knew I was expected. He tied my feet together, as I tried to resist. He hit me with another stomach punch.

"You're a slow learner, Dougay." Mentally I agreed with him. I wanted to say that out loud, but he whipped a gag through my teeth and tied it behind my head. He pulled together my hands and tied them effortlessly at my chest. Defeated, I lay back appreciating his seaman's skill with knots.

He left, locking the door from the outside.

"Sorry about the violence." I looked at Ms Walton. She'd been in the cabin all the time. She came and sat on the bunk next to me as if I were a child recovering in hospital and she was Florence Nightingale—though I couldn't tell if Florence's spirit had come here from Heaven or Hell.

Overhead, I heard footsteps—quite a bit of movement in fact. Three or four people up there were moving down the ladder and I heard and felt some of them step off the boat.

Ms Walton touched my brow with the back of her hand as if checking I had a fever. Her touch was surprisingly gentle. I almost felt she cared. "Just relax. You only need to be like this for a short time."

There was a knock at the cabin door. It opened from the outside. My caring nurse crossed to it. I heard Kempenski's voice. "Enjoy the weekend. I'll see you back in New York."

"I'll come up on deck with you. Wave you all goodbye." I understood at last her New Jersey accent. She left the cabin. The door was locked again.

I heard Matty shout, "Don't forget this!" There followed muffled sounds, then he shouted, "Have a safe flight!"

It would not have been more than minutes that I lay there, before the boat's engines turned over. We moved slowly off, gathering pace, then settled into a cruising speed. After a time, I knew we were well and truly out of Cannes harbour and powering on open water. I began to wonder over the centuries of conflict, how many corpses rested on the bottom—and how long it would be before I joined them.

The cabin door opened. Matty came in and stood to one side. Ms Walton followed him. Matty untied the gag. I breathed with relief. As he untied my feet, he said, "Don't try and kick me. If you do, I'll hit you where it hurts like hell."

"I hope that won't be necessary," said the cold-hearted woman. I didn't move. I didn't doubt Matty would. I pushed my feet forward, getting some movement back into my ankles. He untied my hands. I rubbed my wrists.

Ms Walton sat by my side again. "Now, for dinner would you like seafood?"

"What? I eat it, or you toss me overboard and it eats me?"

She opened the door and let Matty out. She sat on the bunk again.

I looked in her eyes and spoke seriously, "Are you aware that you've assaulted me, kidnapped me and kept me prisoner?" She smiled back. "Are you aware of the crimes you've just committed? Ms Walton?"

She took hold of my hand. "Call me Mary-Anne. Think of this as an early birthday gift—a magical mystery tour, all expenses paid."

It's hard staying mad for long with your kidnapper when she asks you to be on a first-name basis with her and she offers you lobster for dinner, accompanied by a white Bordeaux and afterwards cold beers swilled up on the top deck, gently floating on the Mediterranean with the lights of the Riviera as backdrop.

The skipper had anchored in the late afternoon in a bay, sheltered not far from shore. Leaving Cannes, we'd headed towards Monaco. This bay was beyond there—perhaps in Italy. I had no idea—I'd never seen the Riviera from this angle.

It was well past seven when I realised Milovic would be drinking slivovitz without me tonight.

After he had apologised many times for hitting me, Matty had served the drinks and Mary-Anne had prepared the feast, for that's what it was. Perhaps it had been catered for on shore and all she had to do was remove the plastic wrapping.

The skipper and Matty bid us 'good night' and went below. I rested my head back and looked at the stars overhead.

"Don't go to sleep, just yet," she said in a voice which once again had lost its sharpness. She was back being the woman I'd had dinner and drinks with last night.

"Aren't you curious as to why?" she asked in her New Jersey accent. It made me smile, though I didn't say anything. "Dougay, I believe you may have one more dot to join." She had me curious now. I watched her walk down below. She returned with two opened beers. She handed both to me.

"What final dot? What do you mean?" I asked sipping from one.

She stood before me and slipped her dress over her head. She only wore a red silk G-string. She may have been slightly older than me, but like Francine before her, her body packed a powerful punch. She turned around. There was a small *fleur-de-lis* tattooed on her right buttock.

Chapter 23

Mary-Anne was in no hurry to put her dress back on. "You don't mind, do you?" she asked, casually.

"No," I stammered, "No, not at all."

"It's just that I get so little opportunity to be my real self. We all play a game, don't we, Dougay? I need to get out of mine once in a while. Like last night. 'Ms Walton, assistant production secretary to Mister Harold Kempenski' can be a very restraining position to maintain for every waking moment." I nodded, appreciating her candour—and her beauty.

"Aren't you going to ask me?" she enquired. "I know you want to."

"Ask you what?" I lied. I was desperate to know.

"How I came to get the *fleur-de-lis*."

"Is that what it is?" I lied again. She must have been having an impact upon me. I never lie to a woman—only when I'm falling in love with her. It's some kind of parachute—you know, soften the blow of landing when she tells you to get lost.

Mary-Anne laughed at me. "You asked about it last night. Remember?" Sometimes when you play dumb, you can trip over yourself. I changed the subject.

"Whose idea was this—this very pleasant kidnapping? Kempenski? DeMarko?"

"Pierre Legrande," she said, simply. "He said to stop you interrupting the flow and to treat you like a king. He said you'd left in such a temper—he feared for what you'd do."

I had no idea what she meant by 'interrupting the flow'. Why would he not want some kind of retribution on Calvin deMarko after learning he'd killed Danielle? I didn't understand that. Maybe I was more Australian than French, after all.

"Yes, I was one of Pierre's father's special girls, who grew up and was helped into the position you now see me in. It's true what Pierre would have told you. He does look after his girls. He manages to place them in a solid career after their working life is over. Maybe employed by the men they once serviced or even marrying them. Oh, I never serviced Mister Kempenski. I acquired this job through a friend of a friend of a friend. There's no sexual relationship between Harold Kempenski and me. I have no idea what his sexual preferences are."

I knew.

"Can I get you another beer?" I asked, rising from the deck chair.

"Yes—please."

I went below deck. *Kempenski's sexual preferences?* I thought.

"Pubescent and preferably unbroken," I muttered to no one. I'd answered my own question. I felt my stomach tighten, recalling that blood-stained mattress in the back of Remy's truck; the truth Serge had told us in the third-rate café, concerning the stocky American and the virgin.

I took the two beers back up on deck. I handed one to Mary-Anne.

She sipped her beer. She wanted to clarify something; I could tell. "The business practise—helping us—'aging women'—was established by Pierre's father. Pierre merely inherited a successfully set up operation."

"You knew his father," I said, "And I know his mother."

"Yes, I believe so," said Mary-Anne. "A lovely, dignified woman—she actually loved him. A pity he cheated on her." I looked enquiringly at her. "Not with me. Francine was his favourite."

I sat there stunned. Mary-Anne noticed. "Are you cold? I'll get you a blanket." She went below deck. I watched the *fleur-de-lis* disappear and lifted my beer towards it in a toast. Was the Francine she mentioned, 'my Francine'? I tried to recall the times I'd seen Francine naked. I had always seen her in the dark, her body silhouetted in her window, back lit by the cold blue street light. I'd held it, clutching her to my body as if she was some life force and I was pushing her energy into me, trying to keep my dying body alive. However, like everyone, I was unable to see with my fingertips.

Mary-Anne returned with a blanket, herself wrapped in a second one. "Oh, how disappointing," I said.

"Tomorrow," she said, "I'll let you see it all again. There's a sandy beach over there—deserted—and we can swim there all day if you like."

"I like."

She placed the blanket over me and whispered, "I truly enjoyed our evening together last night." She sat again.

I waited for her to settle. I asked, "This Francine—who's she?"

"The lawyer, who employed you to deliver the screenplay." I waited for her to say, 'The lawyer who you satisfied on Friday evenings, until you tried too hard and thought you'd fallen in love with and frightened her off.' But she didn't—Mary-Anne didn't know anything about that.

"Yes, the screenplay," I said, nodding, remembering. I was remembering out loud for her, not for me. I was never going to forget.

"We start shooting it when I get back. It's been fast-tracked. There are great expectations for *Au revoir, Mate!*"

"What?" The evening was full of surprises. "I don't recall it being called that!"

"No. I loved the last line so much, with its cynicism and off-handedness, that I suggested to Kempenski he change the title. With the money we paid him, Phillips couldn't have cared less."

"Of course not! Why would he?" I protested. "The final line of that script was mine!"

She looked at me and then laughed. "Well, all you're going to need is another hundred and fifty pages and you'll have a screenplay!" She laughed again. Peeved, I drained my beer.

We sat and let the evening air bring on sleep. I awoke in a cabin downstairs. Mary-Anne whispered, "Again. I love it pre-dawn."

We spent the Sunday, as she'd suggested, on the beach. After breakfast Matty had prepared a picnic hamper, and the four of us had gone ashore. Sometime in the afternoon, he and the skipper disappeared behind a rock down the end of the small cove and Mary-Anne told me how up until last night, she'd never really had naturally willing sex. Wasn't that something like Francine had said to me, when she first propositioned me? Was that a line these special girls developed in later life? I hoped not.

That night in her cabin, locked together, she stopped my motion, by holding me, hugging me firmly, as if she didn't want to let me go. I lifted my head. She had a small tear falling down her left cheek. I went to brush it away. "No," she said. "Leave it there. I've never cried for a man before."

*

Monday morning, Milovic's car was where it always was. I lifted Mary-Anne's large suitcase into the trunk and he drove to the airport. On the way there, Mary-Anne and I sat in the back seat holding hands as if we were on a first date. She whispered to me that she'd like to pick up with me again when she returned next year. I made out I believed her. Then she handed me her mobile number and I thought it just might be.

Milovic took the 'Departures' ramp and pulled over into the drop-off area. I went around the back and heaved out her suitcase. I joined her on the footpath to the side of the entrance, allowing many people to brush by, though I didn't see any of them.

She kissed me, passionately, and said intimately, "I want to believe I can have someone to believe in at last."

I held her back from me and looked deep into her eyes. "So do I."

"It's going to be a long cold winter," she whispered. "If anyone comes your way, take them to bed, but don't fall in love with them."

"There's little chance of that happening," I knew I had no intention of doing so.

"Be here, waiting for me—okay?" She ran her hand down my cheek. It felt as soft as the time I was tied up on the bunk, gagged, and she checked my brow. When was that? Only two days ago!

She rubbed her nose across mine. "Back in New York, I'm going to view some Australian films. I want to understand you a bit better."

"I'm French!"

"Yeah, right—sure you are," she said in her broadest New Jersey accent.

"Do you really want me to wait for you?" I needed reassuring. Before a firing squad I'd need to know the guns weren't loaded with blanks.

"If you can't trust an old call girl, who can you trust?" She dragged her suitcase inside the terminal. I stood watching her disappear into the crowd and wondered if she'd meant that seriously or not. I hoped she'd meant it seriously.

Automatically I climbed into the rear seat of Milovic's limousine.

"What you doing back there?" asked a surprised Milovic. "Come—you sit up here with the rest of us workers."

I climbed out and into the front seat. Milovic drove off.

"Mother of God," he said, "Now I know why you didn't turn up on Saturday night. You sleep with her over the weekend?"

"Milovic, a gentleman never divulges such things."

He laughed out loud and slapped the steering wheel. "You did! You did! The slivovitz is on me!"

Chapter 24

By the time Autumn arrived, the tourists had left. The Cannes Festival and all its hype was a memory. Stars had walked the red carpet. Mere mortals had gushed, held back by security guards and a flimsy silver coated chain. Films had been screened and judged and prizes had been handed out. Cameras had clicked and videoed and reporters from all over the world had commented excitedly into them.

I missed it all—I was unable to get time off work. Claude was inflexible when it came to his irregular offers of employment.

M'sieur Pom told me that Belinda Swann had been expected to make an appearance, present an award, however at the last minute had to withdraw. He said that the media had said that it was 'a scandal' and that all the organisers were up in arms. I figured she'd be fearful of showing her face in town for some time, now that *I* knew what she had been up to. Yes, for a moment, I like to big note myself.

Madame Legrande said the real reason Belinda Swann didn't show was that her husband was filming and she, being a truly supportive wife, wished to stay close by him. I didn't buy that and I didn't deny it in Madame Legrande's presence.

Mary-Anne had called to tell me she wouldn't be coming to Cannes for the festival. I hadn't been aware she'd been considering it. She was deep in production of *Au Revoir, Mate!* Calvin deMarko was being his usual demanding, self-centred asshole self, on set. The glamour couple were home in America, way out of my reach, safe in the embrace of Hollywood, protected by its spider's web of clinging minions.

Harold Kempenski had flown in for the festival, walking the red carpet with some gorgeous film starlet on his arm. M'sieur Pom told me she had 'wonderful teeth' and that she smiled a lot—probably realising that at the age of seventeen she was far too old for him.

Madame Legrande, on our favourite park bench, confided in me, "In my day, Dougay, we women were far more appealing—we had class. Oh, the years Sophia Loren was in charge. What a wonderful time! All whores today, all whores!"

For me, the highly paid work dried up. Nothing exciting came my way which involved super yachts; crashing down doors to take a photograph of a fornicating couple; or girls with a *fleur-de-lis* tattooed on their smooth, tanned ass.

Claude asked if I could come by each afternoon around four and wash up and clean in the kitchen. For the autumn and winter, he was not opening at night and Marcel had gone home to Marseilles to nurse his ill mother. I was grateful to him, for the money he paid me covered my weekly food bill. Also, he said I could eat any of the leftover cake and croissants he hadn't sold that day. I began to save money, money I could spend on my planned renovation. Though after a time, I grew tired of cake and croissants.

One morning I stopped in front of my 'memorial wall to Danielle Hubert'. I took the pins out and tossed away her photos. I now wanted to remember her alive and happy. I drew a pencil through the word 'toothpicks', and hoped those two assholes had been inconvenienced enough. If they hadn't, I still had plenty more of the thin wooden sticks in the kitchen cupboard.

Remy called to tell me he'd got his hand on several boxes of large wall tiles with matching smaller ones for the floor. He thought they might be suitable for my bathroom. He gave me a good price—what in Australia we call 'mate's rates'. He let me borrow a trolley and gave me some heavy-duty cardboard boxes. He said he'd been back up in the hills behind Eze with that excellent Bordeaux and stayed the weekend. I couldn't believe it! He laughed at me, "Gotcha!" I was back playing straight man.

I spent the first few days chipping away the old tiles and filling the boxes. Placing them on the trolley, I wheeled it to the elevator and on the ground floor. M'sieur Pom held the doors open while I struggled out into the foyer with them. I then wheeled them around the back of the building. M'sieur Pom assisted by regularly sweeping up any mess which I had dropped on his immaculately kept floor of irreplaceable marble.

When I had enough boxes stacked out there, I'd call Remy and he'd drop by with his truck and under the cover of darkness, we'd dump the rubble somewhere out of the way. He was an old hand at this—he never dumped the load in the same place twice. I saw at night a lot of the Riviera I never knew existed.

For a new arrival I was fortunate—I had a motley crew about me, who were kind, helpful and fast becoming 'family'. I felt I was at last 'settling in'.

The walls and floor of my bathroom weren't water tight. I spent some money and applied a waterproofing to the floor and after it dried, I mixed six bags of concrete and spread it in a thin layer.

I replaced the two walls which came to a join behind the shower with sheets of waterproof cladding—courtesy of a friend of a friend that Remy knew. I painted the ceiling with three coats. Three coats, not two, because it's backbreaking painting overhead and I didn't want to stand there with a roller on a broom handle for many years to come. I set about tiling the floor and walls.

One of the cartons was labelled, 'Happy Birthday, Dougay'. It wasn't my birthday. I opened it anyway. It contained maroon border tiles.

"Thanks, Remy, a thoughtful touch," I said to him over the phone.

"Thoughtful? Me? Not me. A woman from America rang to ask what you would really like to have. I told her. She told me to go buy them for you. She overcompensated me, Dougay."

"Yes, she's done that to me as well!"

"Don't lose that one. She sounds classy—and I look forward to more tips!"

The next day another friend of Remy's, unannounced, knocked on my door with a diamond headed electric tile cutter. He set about cutting the tiles to complete the joins between the top of the walls and the ceiling—and the fiddly little bits needed to fit around the floor waste. As mysteriously as he'd arrived, he'd left.

I removed the matchsticks from the wall tiles and applied the grout. The next day I wiped it all down with a damp cloth. I wondered if it was the same cloth with which I'd cleaned Eloise's scratches.

Scouring through Remy's warehouse, I found a large square showerhead and matching chrome taps. "Take them, they're yours." Remy was becoming generous.

"Thanks. I thought I saw my name written on them."

"Mmm," was all he said. I should have been wary.

"You wouldn't happen to have a good quality porcelain toilet back there, anywhere, would you?"

He considered my request. "I'll need you to give me a hand on Sunday. Be here at 7 am—can't tell you anymore. It's dodgy—but we don't have to kill anyone." He needed a favour in return. He wasn't that generous after all.

When I'd finished the renovation, I stood back and admired my beautiful, light grey with black streaked tiled wet room, circled by a maroon border. It was first class. I remembered Eloise had seen my apartment. I'm sure now she wouldn't rate me as being poor.

I thought I'd better celebrate my bathroom's completion with Remy. I walked over, on my well-worn route. I banged on the roller door. Remy opened the single steel one.

"It's finished!" I said joyously. "Want to come around and have a celebratory shower with me?"

He looked askance. I burst out laughing. "Who's the straight man, now?" I asked gleefully.

As thanks for all Remy had done for me, I took him to Vlatava-Elbe, and with Milovic, we had a night on the slivovitz. An hour after arriving there, my mysterious tile-cutter turned up and I converted him to the joys of the plum liqueur. Three days after, Remy called to thank me for the wonderful evening and to say his hangover had finally left him.

On Sunday morning, if there was a spot of sun in Place Mozart, I'd sit out there and be joined by Madame Legrande. The first morning she told me of the time she kissed Charles Aznavour. I thought she was mistaken—I recalled she'd kissed Yves Montand. But no. Over the weeks I learnt she'd also kissed Gilbert Becaud; Alain Delon and Jean-Paul Belmondo. When she'd go back inside, she'd kiss me. Clearly the old woman had taste.

Not too deep into the change of season, she carried a plastic shopping bag to our regular meeting spot. She sat and took out of it a hand-knitted scarf. She presented it to me. I was overwhelmed. I told her, "The only one who ever knitted me a scarf was a girlfriend, back in Sydney, who promptly went off and married another man."

"I won't leave you," she said, slyly. I was becoming the straight man for everyone.

Each time she kissed me goodbye, I always remembered Francine kissing me, then closing her apartment door. I remembered often our Friday nights. I'd pushed too hard there. I now knew that I should have kept my distance, played by her rules. I'd thought I'd fallen for the lady and wanted more. I was a victim of my own greed.

And with that in mind, I decided to take my time with Mary-Anne. It's a cliché but one door does close and another door does open. I didn't know if it was only going to be ajar or wide open.

Francine still occasionally called for me to deliver a document, however nothing that needed my fists to reinforce a signature. Most of the time, the papers were waiting with the young receptionist. It was now 'strictly, strictly business' as Francine had said. I was content with that.

Once I saw her picture in the social pages—a lawyer's ball or something—and she was standing arm in arm happily smiling with a grey-haired man I thought I vaguely recognised. I showed the picture to M'sieur Pom.

"Fine-looking woman," he said. I pointed to the gentleman. "Oh, that's the mayor, Maurice St Romain—never to be threatened by the aspirations of ex-Deputy Mayor Deschamps again. From memory the Mayor is somehow related to the first family of Monaco."

Like all cities of wealth, there were those who lived a life above the common throng. A world propped up by money and contacts and family ties and breeding. A world which people like me can only enter and linger briefly. While there we get to observe. Some of us get to remember. The sane ones, like Milovic, take the money and go and forget. Me—I entered and observed and even though I took some of the money, I left with a taste in my mouth for a bit more of that world. Ah well, life's long and you never know who or what is on the other end of a phone call.

I'd been back in France, the land of my birth, for around six months and what had I achieved? Not much. I was still alive—which is something a single, unkept and uncared for man of my age should not underestimate.

Now I'd returned, did I feel 'French'? I couldn't say. Maybe I'll always be a hybrid—speaking French with an irrefutable Australian attitude to life and those around me living it.

When alone on the park bench in Place Mozart, I'd often question what I had tried to solve and why. I'd solved nothing for Eloise—she always knew who'd scratched her and tried to choke her and dumped her ignominiously onto the footpath outside my apartment block. She'd taken the money and forgotten. I'd solved it for Pierre who'd, after so much interest, dropped it like a hot potato. I'd solved it for his brother, *le flic*. He'd let it go cold. It was my moral outrage, not theirs, which had driven me. Yes, selfishly, I'd tried to solve it for me. However, I also believed, I'd tried to solve it for Danielle.

I thought of Mary-Anne Walton. I thought of her a lot. I thought of the similarities she had with Francine—organised, self-knowing, self-assured, and not needing any person to interfere with her life. Loneliness was not yet an issue for either of them. And every time I thought of Mary-Anne, I tried convincing myself that she wouldn't be back for the summer. However, more often than not, I convinced myself she would be and I'd be the first one waiting to hear her robin's song.

I heard a plane overhead and looked up. I thought of the Hollywood glamour couple up there, looking back down at us little people. I thought of myself, tied up on the yacht, hearing their plane climbing overhead and them closing another chapter of their depraved life. I feared for their next victim.

It's another cliché, I know. You can tilt at all the windmills you want, and rarely do they topple.

My mobile rang. It was Mary-Anne. Was summer here already? No, she was ringing from New York.

"How'd the filming go?" I asked eagerly, wishing to hear her voice.

"It was a rushed job—we're finished, three days ago—but guess what?"

"What?"

"Calvin deMarko is dead. Killed last night in a car crash—hit by a truck—three days after filming wrapped. Just like James Dean!"

She spoke of other things; people I had no idea of; film locations I'd vaguely heard of; and all the while I was only interested in whether she was happy and safe. *Am I becoming her father?* I joked to myself. I wished her well and told her I couldn't wait to catch up with her in the summer.

I hung up and sat there. A text arrived from Mary-Anne. It read: *I get a kick out of you.* I tapped the attachment. Sinatra sang the Cole Porter song. I listened. I would listen to it many times heading towards my first winter in Nice.

Calvin deMarko dead?

Later that evening, I sat in Place Mozart. A car pulled up and Pierre Legrande alighted—wrapped in a fake fur coat—or was it real? If it was, then only he'd have the audacity to wear such an environmentally incorrect item. He went inside to visit his mother. After twenty minutes or so, I saw him walk back to the front desk and ask something of M'sieur Pom. The old man pointed out the door.

Pierre crossed the narrow street and sat beside me. "That's exactly where your mother sits," I said.

"Nice scarf," he replied, knowingly.

He put his hand on my knee. "I have to apologise for the welcome you received on *The Blue Dahlia*." I said nothing. "Though, I do believe, that the entire weekend was most satisfactory." I eased back and took his eye. "She never listened to my father, when it came to things of a personal nature. Mary-Anne is her own woman. She has been for a very long time." I nodded, taking it in. "She is also a very honest woman—believe what she says."

I waited for him to go on. "I couldn't have you getting in the way—messing up my plans—you understand?" I didn't understand. He changed the subject. "My mother enjoys her chats with you."

"I think I enjoy them more than she does."

"Did she tell you she once kissed President Mitterand?"

"No!" I laughed. "She has such a wonderfully diverse collection of scalps." My laughter died and Pierre let it, before going on.

"Terrible news out of America," he said. "It appears Calvin deMarko was killed in a head-on collision with a truck." He took a thick envelope out of his pocket. "No worthwhile decision was ever made in haste, Dougay. I have tentacles and they reach into the United States. There are many truck drivers who are looking for an extra bit of cash. Dougay—never shit in your own backyard."

Leaving the envelope on my knee, he returned to the car which drove off.

I sat for a long time; the envelope balanced there perfectly. I thought of everything I'd been through since I picked Eloise up from the footpath just over there in front of me.

I held my hand in the shape of a gun, as Philip J. Phillips had done on the promenade. I imagined Calvin de Marko's face on the cover of a film magazine. As Mary-Anne had told me, with cynicism and off-handedness, pulling the trigger, I said, "*Au revoir, mate!*"